CALM UNDONE

A Novel

GARTH A. FOWLER

BQB

North Carolina

Published in the United States by BQB Publishing
(an imprint of Boutique of Quality Books Publishing, Inc.)
www.bqbpublishing.com

978-1-952782-18-3 (p)
978-1-952782-19-0 (e)

Library of Congress Control Number: 2021941865

Book design by Robin Krauss, www.bookformatters.com
Cover design by Rebecca Lown, www.rebeccalowndesigns.com

First editor: Andrea Vande Vorde
Second editor: Allison Itterly

For my family

For many years my grandmother rented a house in Stone Harbor, New Jersey, and for two weeks my whole family—siblings, cousins, aunts, and uncles—would descend upon the shores. Long before she died, we all grew up and went our separate ways. But those years we spent at the beach house made us a family.

Chapter 1

Before Dad died, we would all spend the summer at the beach. Mom and I would leave sometime after school had ended, and then Dad would fly out for long weekends. At the end of August, he would come stay for his two weeks of vacation before we would all head back home to Chicago together. When it was time for Dad to join us, he would work the night before and then take the red-eye, arriving at the beach house early the next morning. He always came straight to my room and woke me up so we could watch the sun rising over the beach together.

"Tyler," he would say, shaking me gently. "Tyler. Come on. Let's go." When I was still young, he would pull me from underneath my covers and hold me in his arms, swaying back and forth as I slowly woke up. "Hot chocolate downstairs, buddy. Hurry, it will get cold." He'd set me down on the edge of the bed and disappear through my door. I would search for my hooded sweatshirt, pulling it on over my pajamas and slip downstairs.

In the kitchen, Dad poured hot chocolate into his thermos. Then we headed outside and down the street to the beach. Sprinklers turned on and off as we walked past the immaculate lawns. I loved how the air smelled of salt and fresh-cut grass and the way the sun just peeked over the dunes at the end of the street. When we reached the beach, Dad opened his thermos and took a deep whiff of the steam rising out of it. He was a connoisseur of foods, always smelling and tasting. After smelling the chocolate in the thermos, he poured some in the cap and handed me the rest. I smelled it too, imitating what he did. I closed my eyes and inhaled fast and deeply, puffing out my chest and filling my lungs. A rich and sweet scent danced through my nose and then was gone. I tried to imagine what it was we were smelling, but I never asked him. I wanted him to think I knew.

As the tide moved in, Dad and I would stand side by side and watch the ocean crashing hard against the sand, frothing and foaming as it slowly advanced toward us. I nursed my chocolate—Dad always made me too much, and so early in the morning it was too sweet and heavy for my stomach. With both hands wrapped around the thermos, I crunched the sand between my toes, squeezing it tightly until my calves strained. The seagulls flew above us. They always knew when we had food. Sometimes I shouted at them or waved my arms to scare them away. But Dad put his hand on my arm. "Let them be," he said. So I would.

After the sun came up and we finished our hot chocolate, we went back to the house where Dad made breakfast as I napped on the couch. He prided himself in his pancakes. "The best buckwheat pancakes the world over," he told me as he slid a plate in front of me. "Take your time. Not everyone gets to eat these. Savor them." Then he sipped his coffee and read the New Yorker as I ate.

I loved being up early with Dad more than I loved the pancakes.

My freshman year I joined the high school cross-country team. I was surprised at how good I was and how much I liked it. What I'd always thought to be a curse of being skinny and gangly was suddenly a gift. I was thin and lithe, with long legs that were built for long runs. I wasn't the fastest guy on the team, but I held my own. Having been a bit of a loner in junior high, I now had friends on the cross-country team. We weren't the coolest jocks in school, but we were a close group. And I liked being a runner.

During the school year, I ran early each morning by myself on Lake Shore Path. Running along Lake Michigan in Chicago reminded me of being on the beach over the summer: the birds overhead, the sound of the water, the mist in the air. When summer came, I started running along the beach in Stone Harbor. That first summer after I joined the team, Dad arrived at the beach house just as I was getting dressed to run.

"Hey, Marathon Man," he said, appearing at my door.

"Hey," I said, pulling my head through a long-sleeved running shirt. His eyes were dark and heavy looking. His gray slacks were wrinkled, and his red sweater hung from his shoulders. His hair was cut short, and little white hairs stood out against his scalp. He arrived earlier than I had anticipated—I had hoped I would be able to finish my run before he landed. He looked tired, and I felt guilty, thinking he had rushed to see me before the sunrise and I wasn't going to spend it with him.

"How far you going?" he whispered. Even though Mom was down the hall in their room, he would whisper as we talked. He liked the stillness of the morning.

"Three. Maybe four. We'll see."

"No shoes?" He pointed to my bare feet.

I shook my head. I liked the way the sand felt against my bare feet. It would crunch up beneath my toes, just like when I was younger. "Too hard to run in the sand with shoes."

"Oh." He raised his eyebrows and cracked a smile. "Well, let's go. I'll walk down with you."

We walked along the same street, the houses quiet, the lawns still immaculate. Dad carried his thermos. Not knowing

I was running, he had already made hot chocolate for both of us. After that, he stopped making hot chocolate in the thermos and brought with him just a single cup of coffee. I wondered how he felt about that, the change from hot chocolate for two to coffee for one. But I never got to ask.

"Long flight?" I asked.

"Always," he laughed.

"Get everything done before you left?"

"Never, but that doesn't matter. People will still get their news, both today and tomorrow. And I get to be here with you." Dad was the publisher of the Chicago Tribune, making sure the company hit its targets for the number of readers and revenue from advertisements. As a rule, the beach house had no television. When he was here with us, he'd say, he was all ours.

We reached the beach and he sipped his coffee. The waves attacked and retreated, and the wind ruffled my shirt against my chest. I jumped up and down and swung my arms in the air, trying to get my heart rate up. Once I felt ready to spring, I whispered, "Okay," mostly to myself but loud enough for Dad to hear.

"Go get 'em, killer," Dad said, tousling my curly, chestnut hair. Then I left him, smelling his coffee and watching me as I took off along the water.

Chapter 2

Liam and I sit in beach chairs and watch a group of kids play volleyball. Four girls and four boys, all about our age—sixteen or seventeen. They're mostly goofing around, not keeping score but just trying to keep the ball going back and forth across the net. Whenever someone misses a play or the ball hits the sand, they laugh as if it was the funniest thing that ever happened. "Dive for it!" one of the guys in long shorts yells, and a girl in a pink-and-yellow bikini half jumps, half falls into the sand. She's not even close to the ball, and the group explodes with laughter. Liam watches the entire episode, especially the girl. She is his type—blonde, tanned skin, and petite.

Liam is my cousin. His mother is my aunt Marion, and technically she and Mom own the beach house together. It was their family beach house from when they were little girls. They grew up in Philadelphia, where Grandpa owned a coal mining company and a construction company that did work for the state of Pennsylvania. Their whole family would escape the hot and oppressive Philadelphia summers by packing up and moving to the Jersey Shore. Grandpa bought a four-story beach house in Stone Harbor, a small city on one of the barrier islands almost an hour south of Atlantic City. When he died, before I was even born, Mom and Aunt Marion decided to keep it.

Every summer since I can remember, Mom and I would spend practically the whole summer in Stone Harbor. Aunt Marion and Liam would come down too, but only stay for two or three weeks. Aunt Marion is an artist in Baltimore, selling her paintings and sculptures from a small studio. She has always said she can't afford to close down for the whole summer. They had always overlapped their stay with Dad's, though. It made the beach house feel full and fun.

Liam and Aunt Marion have been here for almost two weeks, trying to fill the void that Dad's death has left. Dad died almost six months ago, but Mom insisted that we still spend the summer here. To be honest, I didn't want to come here. I couldn't imagine being here without him. But Mom insisted. "Aunt Marion and Liam are coming too, for the whole summer." And that was the end of the discussion.

Without a choice in the matter, I decided to try to use this summer to remember as much about Dad as I could. Not long after he died, I started having nightmares that I forgot his name or what he looked like. I figured Liam and I could do all the things that Dad used to do with us: visit the wetlands and bird preserve, rent a boat to go crabbing, or fish off one of the piers on the east side of the island. But we haven't done any of that.

Instead, Liam and I have been filling our mornings and afternoons on the beach, and spending the evenings downtown at the small arcade and putt-putt golf stands. Sometimes we just sit on the porch, playing cards, talking about school. Liam and I will both be seniors this fall. He plays lacrosse, and scouts from major colleges are already making plans to come watch him play next spring. I got to see him play last summer and when he walked out on the field with all the other players I almost laughed. He was shorter than the other players, and his unruly red hair jutted out of the vents of his helmet. But he's aggressive and plays hard. He never backed down from any of the other players and scored three goals.

"Are you still going to run cross-country?" he asks, his eyes never leaving the group of kids playing volleyball.

"Sure," I lie. I haven't run in months, although I often would put on my gear and leave the house.

"I thought we could go to the kite shop tonight." Liam turns his gaze from the blonde to me. "Is that okay with you? I mean, if you don't want to, then we can do something else."

Instead of answering, I get up and head to the bathroom. I don't really have to go. This is my way of escaping that question: Is it okay? Going to the kite shop is not okay. It is torture. The kite shop was one of Dad's favorite places. He loved the colors and the fact that there were so many different shapes and sizes— box kites, sled kites, and the common diamond. I never got why he liked it so much. We never bought a kite, but we couldn't walk past it without him dragging all of us inside. After Mom said we were coming here this summer, it was one of the places I thought about the most. Part of me wants to go. Part of me also knows that all I will do is miss him when I'm there.

And the second question about wanting to do something else is even more stupid because it means I should find something that won't make me think of Dad. Every time someone asks me if I want to avoid doing something that might make me miss Dad, I feel like they are trying to get me to pretend he was never alive. Act like he never came to the beach house, or watched the sunrise with me, or made us pancakes. But I keep all of this to myself.

The bathroom floor is cold against my bare feet. If I stay in here too much longer, Liam will come looking for me, asking if I am okay. I splash some water on my face, dry my hands on my swimming suit, and walk back toward our chairs. By the time I get back, Liam has joined the volleyball game. One of the girls is sitting on the side, so the teams are even with Liam playing. He's on the team opposite the blonde in the bikini, but he's trying hard to impress her. He has his shirt off and makes a point of saving bad plays.

Finally, the lifeguards blow their whistle, indicating it is five o'clock and the beaches are closed. As the other teens gather up their stuff, Liam talks briefly with the girl in the bikini. She claps excitedly at something he says, and then joins the rest of her friends. Liam comes over to me as I fold up our chairs.

"We're going to a party tonight," he says. "One of the guys over there—his parents are out of town and he's having people over tonight. Dude, we have to go. If you're okay with that?"

A party would be something different; definitely not anything that would remind me of Dad. But I'm still not sure, so I say nothing. Which Liam takes as a yes.

After we eat dinner with Mom and Aunt Marion, Liam goes upstairs to change. Then he comes down and announces he and I were going to hang out with some friends. We walk down First Avenue, which travels along the beach. Liam has the address of the house written on a small piece of paper. The houses here are bigger than ours, with four-car garages that take up the entire front lawn. Most have backyards that go right up to the beach and large swimming pools in back, which I think is stupid. Why have a swimming pool when you have a beach right outside your window? I guess because you can afford it.

"Dude," Liam whistles. "Makes our place look like a dump, huh?"

"They're just newer, that's all," I say. As we walk up the drive, music pulses from the open windows. A large fence runs around the back of the house, and I hear the sound of kids laughing and jumping into a pool. Liam knocks on the door. Nothing happens. "I guess we can ring the bell," I say.

"Screw that." Liam grabs the knob and swings the door open. Inside, people are milling about, drinks in hand. Some look our way as we close the door and walk in, but no one bothers to greet us. Some of the kids are our age: still in high school, probably starting senior year in the fall. Some look older—one wears a Rutgers sweatshirt, and a couple of guys wear matching dark blue T-shirts with Greek letters. The music is jarring, the bass pounding against my chest. Liam taps my shoulder and leads me to the bottom of the stairwell where it's just a bit quieter.

"What was the girl's name?" I ask.

"Melissa," Liam says, looking around.

"Melissa what?"

"Don't know. Just Melissa. But I'll know her when I see her."

Kids are sitting on the steps, telling stories and drinking from plastic cups. Upstairs I glimpse people running back and forth in front of the stairwell, laughing and dancing. One boy stops at the top of the stairs and throws a beach ball down the steps, hitting the kids below. I don't know why, but it bothers me. Someone turns up the music in the living room and everyone starts to sing along. Liam says something else, but the singing drowns out his words.

I cup my hand to my ear. "What?"

Liam points to the red cups everyone is holding and mouths "drinks." I nod. We go through a dining room and find our way to the kitchen. I stand still for a second, shocked at how much quieter the kitchen is compared to the other room. My ears stop ringing, and the light is brighter here. The noise and chaos are making me anxious, so I'm relieved it's calmer here. The kitchen is empty except for one guy who is leaning against the counter with a red cup in his hand. He wears a tight green T-shirt and a pair of faded baggy jeans. He's thin, but his shoulders and chest are wide and solid looking.

"Hey," Liam calls out. "Drinks in here?"

The guy nods. "Coke and Sprite are on the porch, through there." He points at the glass door that leads to a deck.

Liam starts toward the glass door. "Hey, thanks," he says, and looks over his shoulder at me. "Ty, you coming?"

Just then the blonde girl from the volleyball game comes through the door and into the kitchen. She is wearing white pants and a tank top that makes her tan even more noticeable. A thin, gold chain holds a small, blue stone that matches her eyes. She gives Liam and me a quick smile, but obviously doesn't remember us from before. As she leans against the counter next to the guy, she says, "I've been looking for you, Finn. These guys your friends?" Finn shakes his head and shrugs indicating he doesn't know who we are.

Liam quickly reverses directions and heads back toward the two of them. "You're Melissa, right? We met on the beach today."

"You made it! I didn't recognize you!" Melissa hops up and down, giving a short laugh like I saw her do earlier at the volleyball game. "It's Levi, right? And so, this is your cousin?"

"I'm Liam. And yeah, this is my cousin Tyler."

"That's him?" Melissa asks, bringing both hands up to her mouth. She turns to me and says in a soft voice, "I almost cried when he told me at the beach. I'm so sorry about your dad."

My throat suddenly parches, and my stomach tightens. I snap my head toward Liam. After seeing my reaction, he just stares at his feet. It takes only a second for me to realize that he must have used the accident as a way to get us invited to the party or just talk to Melissa.

"Hey, you want a drink?" Melissa turns to Liam, oblivious to any tension between Liam and me. "Come on, I'll show you where they are." She grabs Liam's hand, and they head through the glass door to the deck.

Finn just quietly sips from his cup. "Melissa's not too subtle," he says after a long silence.

I nod.

Finn slides off the counter and reaches beside me to yank open the door of the fridge. He pulls out a bottle of root beer and, using a key chain shaped like a surfboard, pops the top off before handing it to me. "I'm not much of a Coke or Sprite man," he says.

"Thanks," I finally say. "Is she your friend?"

Finn rolls his head, cracking his neck and closing his eyes. "Kind of. We met about a year ago on the beach. Her family spends the summers here, and we started hanging out. It's hard to say. I only see her during the summer."

The glass door slides open and a boy in a baseball cap rushes in, laughing, and runs around the marble-top island in the middle of the kitchen. A girl follows in after him, dripping wet.

"Greg," she coos. "Greg, come here."

He laughs and shakes his head.

"You are so dead!" she screams, and Greg pushes past Finn and me and runs into the living room. The girl runs past us, splashing water everywhere. Finn hops back up on the counter and grabs a towel to try to dry the front of his pants.

"You live here?" I ask.

"Yeah," he responds, still dabbing his pants.

"Nice." I look around the kitchen, taking it all in.

"What?" Finn looks up. "Oh, yeah. No, not here. Not this house. What about you, you from Philadelphia?"

I shake my head. "Chicago."

"Huh, I thought everyone who came here for the summer was from Philadelphia."

"How do you know I just spend the summers here?"

A sly smile creeps across his face. "There are only like eight hundred people who actually live here. You kind of know who is and isn't from out of town."

"You live in Stone Harbor, not on the mainland?" I ask.

"Yeah."

"What that's like? I mean, is it dead in the winter?"

"Pretty much. The summer gets crazy. But the end of summer is the best. The weather is usually still nice in September, and everyone is gone by then. You can surf all you want with no one bothering you. It gets pretty boring in the winter, but then I hang with people from school. You know, the usual stuff, I guess."

I look out the glass door and wonder where Liam is.

Finn follows my gaze and laughs. "I think they forgot your drink," he says as he tosses the towel he used to dry his lap into the sink. "So, your cousin, Liam. He usually ditch you for girls like that?"

"No," I say taking my first sip. "First time, to tell the truth."

Chapter 3

In the crash I broke my foot, my arm, and two bones in my hand. All on the right side of my body, which was weird because the impact was mostly on the driver's side of the car.

Dad and I were driving up Lake Shore Drive in January. It was one of those unusually warm winters, and there was little snow in Chicago but lots of rain. We were on our way to Evanston to a Baptist church. The Tribune had done a feature about the rate of kidney failure in adults. It was a long series of articles, and the reporter selected four people to follow for two months. One of the subjects was a man named Jimmy who owned a limo company. After the article came out, one of his former employees and a fellow church member decided to donate one of her kidneys to him. She wanted to make the announcement in church, and when she told the pastor, he contacted the Tribune. Dad agreed to come and meet his editor and the reporter there. "The paper wanted another chance at a great story," Dad told me, "and to see firsthand how it was changing the lives of the people who read it."

Lake Shore Drive follows Lake Michigan from downtown Chicago to the north neighborhoods. It ends at Hollywood Avenue where it makes a sharp left turn away from the water. Dad and I were approaching the curve, and he slowed down for the light. Suddenly, the car in front of us started to skid as it turned left. Dad slammed on the brakes and turned harder to the left, but it was too late. The front of our car on the passenger's side just clipped the car in front of us and that sent us sliding sideways. A car from behind slammed into us, tumbling our car across the road and into the barricade. We finally stopped rolling right-side up, but then two other cars hit us again on the driver's side.

But I don't remember any of that. Mom eventually told me what had happened while I was still in the hospital. What I do remember was watching the waves from the lake crash onto the beach at Hollywood Avenue and thinking there must be a storm out over Lake Michigan. Then Dad yelled something and honked his horn. That is the last thing I remember of him.

I woke up in a dark room with beige walls. My right arm and hand were in a cast. I tried to yell, "Hello," but nothing came out. My throat was raw and on fire. I craned my neck trying to figure out where I was and saw a call-button looped around the bars at the head of my bed. I had to stretch my free arm above my head and half roll onto my side to reach it. After pushing the button, I dropped back into my pillow, feeling exhausted and fighting the urge to fall asleep again.

"Tyler?" A nurse walked into the room and picked up the clipboard that hung at the foot of my bed. She looked at her watch and wrote something on the chart. "How do you feel? Do you know where you are?" She smiled sweetly and checked my IV.

"Hospital?" I whispered. I was surprised at how hard it was to talk. I coughed and winced at the pain.

"We had to intubate you for the surgery, so your throat is probably going to hurt for a little bit." She took my temperature, then ran her fingers through my hair.

Once she removed the thermometer, I croaked out, "Surgery?"

"You have pins in your arm, wrist, and foot to keep them together as they heal," she said.

I looked down to see that my right foot was air-casted too. My eyes burned, and I let them close. A dry scratchiness ran across the top of my head. I reached up to touch it. A bandage started at my forehead and ran all the way across the top of my head. As I tried to remember what happened, I suddenly thought about Dad.

"Where is my dad?"

The nurse poured water out of a pitcher and put a small cup to my lips. "We've given you something for the pain, and it is going to make you sleepy. Get some sleep, your body needs it. I'm going to call your mom. She will be happy to know you're awake." I took a small sip and wanted to ask again about Dad. But she was right, I was tired and fell asleep.

When I woke up, Mom was asleep in a chair. For some reason I was afraid to wake her. I sat in silence, just watching her breathe. She was motionless, except for the subtle rise and fall of her shoulders. Finally, I whispered, "Hi," and she woke up.

"Hi, sweetie," she smiled. She sat up and leaned forward from her chair, and kissed my cheek. She patted my arm and sighed.

"Is Dad here?" I asked.

"No," she said. "They took him to another hospital after the crash. Downtown, in a helicopter." She squeezed my hand.

"Is he all right?" I asked. I knew by the look on her face what she couldn't say. She shook her head. I closed my eyes, afraid I was going to cry. But my throat was on fire and nothing came out.

"You cut your forehead and the top of your head pretty good, so we stitched that. Thirty-eight stitches, and they're gonna itch and burn like crazy." My doctor was young and had bright eyes that laughed as much as he did. "But don't worry," he chuckled. "You're young, and any scarring will probably fade away. But it will take some time. In six months, the girls will go crazy for you again."

For the two weeks I was there, he visited me every day and asked me how I was. I had a slight concussion and at times was nauseous and even puked. Other than that, I slept a lot. They were still giving me pain medicine, though I really didn't have too much pain, which was fine with me. I just wanted to sleep through all of this and get home again.

The day before I left the hospital, a nurse gave me a sponge bath and washed my head. I sat up in the bed and leaned over a bowl of warm water she'd placed in my lap. Her fingernails were manicured and painted bright pink to match her scrubs. She had a slight southern accent and long black braids in her hair. As she gently scrubbed my body, she talked about how important it was to feel nice and clean when I would be discharged and going home. "I even had your mom bring in some clean clothes for you to change into when we're done." She motioned toward a pile of clothes sitting on the chair beside my bed.

Finally, she said we were done and then she dried me off as best she could and placed the bowl and towel on the stand beside my bed. She held a mirror behind her back and asked, "You ready, honey?"

I hadn't looked at myself since I'd arrived. I nodded. She hesitated as she held the mirror in front of me. I reached out and took it from her so I could see better. My eyes were black and blue as if I had been punched by a boxer. My thin lips were cut and swollen. The bandage on my head was clean and rectangular and ran at an angle from the left to the right. The cut ran about four inches from my forehead, and they had to shave a line through the middle of my curly hair to keep it out of the stitches.

"Why didn't they just shave it all off?" I rubbed the edges of the bald strip that ran across my scalp.

"It doesn't look that bad." The nurse patted my arm and then gave it a gentle squeeze. She blinked back tears, then started to gather the towels and bowl of water. "And remember what the doctor said: before long, you won't even know this ever happened."

The hospital gave me a pair of crutches, but I wasn't allowed to use them while leaving the hospital. Instead, an orderly helped me into a wheelchair and took me down to the lobby. Mom and Aunt Marion came to pick me up. Aunt Marion had flown into Chicago two days after the accident, and she and Mom visited me every day I was there. Our car had been totaled, so Mom hired a town car to take me from the hospital to home. When we entered the apartment, it felt lonely and empty. There were flowers everywhere, and on the kitchen table was a stack of cards, some unopened.

Aunt Marion helped me to the couch, and Mom went to the kitchen and made herself a cup of coffee.

"Your coach called. He said the whole team hopes you're well," Aunt Marion said. "Some of the boys wanted to visit you at the hospital, but your mom and I thought it would be better to let you rest instead." She got up and brought me a handful of cards from the kitchen table. "These are yours," she said. I looked through the cards.

"How's Liam?" I asked.

"He's fine. I call him every night. He wanted to know when you were getting home. Want to talk to him tonight when he calls?"

"Sure," I said, but I wasn't sure if I wanted to talk to him.

We sat quietly. The only sound came from the wind blowing against the glass door that led to our deck. It whistled as it leaked in through the cracks and made the glass vibrate like a drum. I leaned back on the couch and closed my eyes. The living room seemed foreign to me. It was as if someone had tried to recreate our living room to look exactly like the one I grew up in. It was too clean and all the furniture looked freshly polished. There were always newspapers and magazines spread around the apartment when Dad was around. He used to sit and read with a cup of coffee, facing the deck and looking out over Lake Michigan. He never finished a cup of coffee, so there were always cold half-empty cups about the apartment. Now they were gone. I figured Aunt Marion had probably cleaned the entire place. There could not be that much else to do when they weren't coming to visit me in the hospital.

"Where are the newspapers? Dad's newspapers?" I looked up and saw Mom standing in the kitchen with her coffee cup.

"I'm going to bed. I'm beat," she said. She came over and kissed me gently on the forehead. "Glad you're home, sweetie." She hugged Aunt Marion, and then left the room. Aunt Marion sat on the couch with me.

"What happened to Dad's newspapers?" I asked again.

"I put them in the office. It was such a mess. For about three days, they all had pictures of the crash and headlines about the accident. A couple of newspapers called asking for pictures for the obituary. I had to ask the Tribune to deal with it all."

"Did they?" I asked.

"Yeah," she said. "They've been great. Your mom hasn't had to deal with any of it."

Dad told me that newspapers often have pre-written obituaries of famous people. When someone died, a staff writer quickly updated the information and the details of the person's death. That way the paper could have a story about the person in print shortly after his or her death.

I doubted a pre-written obituary existed for Dad, which meant Spencer, the Tribune's editor, had to write one for him.

I wanted to ask Spencer what that had been like for him. How did he find out what had happened? Did he have to be the one to tell the rest of the Tribune's staff Dad had died? I wanted to see pictures. I wanted to read what they said about Dad. About the crash. About everything.

Dad's office was up a small set of steps that is set apart from the rest of the living room. There was no way I could get there by myself on crutches. I needed to ask Mom or Aunt Marion for help. I knew neither one would want to, which meant I never got answers to any of those questions.

Chapter 4

Wildwood, New Jersey is situated on a barrier island just off the south Jersey shore. For people spending the summer in Stone Harbor, Wildwood is the nightlife spot. It has a boardwalk, a haunted house, video arcades, and miles of T-shirt shops. Liam and Melissa hold hands, walking down the boardwalk about three feet in front of me. It has been a week since we saw her at the party, and I didn't even know Liam had gotten her number. Since it's Friday, Liam asked if I wanted to go to Wildwood, and I said, "Whatever you want to do." Then he told me that we were also going to meet Melissa. Neither has said more than a few words to me since we met Melissa at the rollercoaster that juts high into the air over the beach. With no plans, we decide to walk the boardwalk and take in the sights.

"When we were little, we use to come here on the last day of our vacation and get T-shirts," Melissa says, pointing to a shop on the corner. "I had one T-shirt for each year starting from when I was in fifth grade." She laughs. "I still have most of them in a box. You should see them; some are so horrible."

"We used to come here a couple of years ago and try to score beer," Liam says. "You remember that, Tyler?" He turns to look at me, but before I can respond, he turns to Melissa. "Never worked, though."

Liam and Melissa continue chatting and even kissing as if no one was watching. I wander aimlessly through the noise and chaos. Little kids run circles around their parents' legs, excited to be at the boardwalk. Junior high kids walk in packs, roughhousing with each other and laughing at their own stories. Wildwood has a tram that runs loops up and down the boardwalk. The only people who really use it are old people. A bored driver sits behind the steering wheel, and two speakers mounted on the front blast the tinny voice of a woman that endlessly repeats, "Watch the tram car, please." As the roller coaster goes rushing by, the screams of the riders swell and then fade away.

We head toward a tattoo and piercing shop so Liam can look at an earring. He has been threatening Aunt Marion to get one before the trip is over. All the guys on the lacrosse team are thinking of getting one—a "solidarity thing," he called it. She would laugh and tell him that Uncle Ben, Liam's dad, would probably pull it out from his earlobe if he ever came home with one. "Does the cross-country team do stupid things like that?" Aunt Marion asked me once. I just shrugged.

As soon as we enter the store, Melissa immediately pulls Liam to the end of the counter where a display case holds a collection of studs and stones. Liam wants a gold stud with a red stone. He thinks it will look cool against his pale complexion and red hair. But Melissa objects to everything he picks out.

"I think you'd look cute with this one," she coos. "It brings out your eyes."

"What do you think, Ty?" Liam asks.

For some reason, I hate that Melissa is here. "I think you should get what you want. I mean, it's your ear." I purposely say it to shut down Melissa, and it works. She just stares intently at the display case while Liam mouths at me, "Dude, what is your problem?"

Liam buys a silver stud with an emerald stone and pays for it with Uncle Ben's credit card, which will only piss him off even more. A girl with jet-black hair and tattoos of ravens on her neck tells him it's a thirty-minute wait before his turn. It seems everyone is getting piercings tonight. As she takes down his name, she looks at me and says, "What about you?"

"I don't do earrings," I say.

She stares into my eyes. "Too bad," she says. "Your eyes are intense. You could pull it off."

I think she's flirting with me, because people don't often mention my looks, unlike Liam whose red hair and bright green eyes get pointed out all the time for being typically Irish. I have dark and curly chestnut hair and hazel eyes with bright specks of blue. We both, however, have pale white skin. So when I blush at her comment, I think it must be obvious. I glance over at Liam and Melissa, but they don't even notice I'm still here.

I pretend to be interested in the anime magazines while Liam gets his ear pierced. Melissa fawns over Liam and holds his hand while the tattooed woman punches a hole into his lobe with a gun.

"What do you think?" Liam asks.

"Does it hurt?" His ear is red and swollen, but I have to admit that it looks good. I'm tempted to ask the tattooed woman what she thinks would work with my eyes, since she mentioned them. But going back now after the comment I made earlier would make me look lame.

"Yeah, a little," he replies. "Actually, it's more just annoying. It throbs a little."

"You've got to stop playing with it," Melissa offers. "Like, when I got my ears pierced, for a couple of days you have to leave it alone."

"Then let's go find something to do. I need to take my mind off it." Liam uses his thumb to wiggle his earlobe.

"Well," Melissa drones, "I am supposed to meet a friend,

down a little further on the boardwalk. We could go do that while we try to figure out what to do next."

"Ty?" Liam asks.

I shrug. "Whatever. Let's just do something."

We head out of the store, and Liam again moves his hand to his ear. Melissa slaps his hand.

"Here," she giggles, and puts his hand in her pocket with hers. "See, now you can't play with it."

As we walk along, I try to come up with a way to get out of here. I can suggest to Liam that he and I need to get back home, which he won't agree to, or I can come up with an excuse to go somewhere else on my own, which is a lie. So I'm stuck.

Melissa stops along one of the piers and tells a story about learning to swim there when she was younger. As I watch the white tops of the waves appear from the blackness and crash on the sand in the distance, a sinking feeling comes over me. Last summer, Dad and I came here, and I ran sprints between the two jetties. It was early in the morning before the lifeguards had even set up. Dad drank his coffee and timed me on his watch. Afterwards, we ate pancakes at a diner before going back home.

"Come on," Melissa says. She pulls Liam by the hand, and I follow as we cross the boardwalk toward a Wild-West-themed shooting gallery. Little kids are leaning against the stand paying quarters to hit little round targets with fake shotguns. When they hit the target, it makes a barmaid drop a tray of beer and a piano player start a verse of "The Entertainer." Behind the counter in a red-striped vest and a felt fedora is Finn.

"Look, I told you I would come," Melissa says as she leans over the counter and gives Finn a quick kiss on the cheek.

"Never doubted it," Finn replies. He puts his elbows on the counter and leans toward us. "Hey, Tyler, how you doing?"

At first, I just nod. Finn smiles and waits for something more, so finally I say, "Fine. Thanks."

"Liam got his ear pierced just now," Melissa coos, and puts her hand on the back of Liam's head.

Finn breaks his gaze with me and looks at Liam. "Nice. Mine's an amethyst. I gotta tell you, it's going to itch like crazy in a couple of days, man." He puts his hand behind his left ear and shows a small, silver stud with a purple stone in it.

"Great. It already hurts. You don't happen to have any aspirin back there or something?"

Finn laughs. "Sorry, no such luck." For a second we all just stand there, quiet and awkward. One of the kids at the far end of the shooting gallery asks Finn for more quarters. Finn nods, and after saying he'll be right back, walks away.

"So," Liam says. "What next?"

"There's a party at my friend Emma's house," Melissa says. "She's from New York or something. Her parents have a place at the end of the boardwalk, but they're up in Atlantic City tonight." Melissa looks at her watch. "It's only nine thirty, so it might be early. But I told her I'd come help set up and stuff."

"Hm . . . okay." Liam shrugs. "Will there be hot chicks? I'm not going unless there are hot chicks," he adds, and laughs at me.

"I'll be there," Melissa coos, and runs her hand down Liam's back.

"What do you say, Ty? You in? Maybe we can get you a girl tonight!"

"Is that all guys think about?" Melissa asks.

"What?" Finn responds, getting back from the end of the counter.

"Sex and girls. But not you, sweetie, you're a perfect gentleman," she quickly adds, and pats his hand with a smile.

"No, of course not." Finn throws his arms up in an innocent gesture. He and Melissa laugh.

"We're heading to Emma's," Melissa updates Finn. "You going to be there?"

"I guess so, after I get off here." He looks at his watch. "In about thirty minutes." Then he turns to me. "Hey, you want to wait and hang out until I'm off? They can go early, and then we can show up later?"

"Great!" Melissa exclaims. "You know Emma's address?"

"No," Finn replies. "But we'll text."

Finn and Melissa talk about the last party at Emma's house. As they chat, Liam shoots me a quick glance and quietly asks, "So, you want to go to this party? Would that be okay with you? Because if not, we can do something else."

I shrug. Honestly, I'm happy to finally be rid of Melissa, even if it's just for a bit. I'm really not too excited about another party full of people I don't know, nor about standing around for thirty minutes at the shooting gallery doing nothing while kids shoot fake guns at mechanized targets. I figure I will probably hang out for ten minutes or so after Liam and Melissa leave and come up with an excuse to head back to the car. Liam can find his own way home, I'm sure.

"Looks like he did it again," Finn says as Liam and Melissa walk away.

"What?"

"Ditch you for the girl." He puts one of the guns back into the holder on the counter. There are still about ten kids shooting guns, and music is constantly going on and off in the background. "But I guess I kind of gave him the easy out. Thanks for hanging around, though. It gets really boring here, you wouldn't believe it."

Finn and I make small talk whenever he isn't getting

someone change or unlocking guns for new customers. At exactly ten o'clock, he turns off the gallery, setting off a barrage of protests and complaints from the patrons who still had shots left in their guns.

"Not my problem. The sign says we close at ten, and it's ten," Finn says stiffly. Without making eye contact, he grabs the guns from their hands and locks them to the counter. It reminds me of this one time when me and Dad came to the boardwalk when I was younger. I was playing games in the arcade, begging for just one more minute before we had to leave. Dad didn't protest. Just before I was done, the power to the games just shut off, and the whole place was suddenly quiet. "She's done, Tiger," Dad said, and then put his arm around my shoulder to lead me to the car.

Finn finally shuts everything down, and by the time he puts the money away and locks up the shooting gallery, it is almost twenty after ten. "This way," he says, and we walk between the shooting gallery and a snow cone shop toward a short, dark doorway. He pulls a key out of his pocket and unlocks the door. The office is narrow and long, running the entire width of the shooting gallery. Pipes and wires run in and out of the walls, obviously leading to the mechanized targets for the gallery on the other side. The back wall has a desk, some lockers, and a board with a list of the weekly shifts and employee names.

"So," Finn says as he takes off his striped vest and shirt, exposing his stomach and chest. He unbuttons his pants, and I think he's going to take them off too. Instead, he pulls a white collared shirt from the locker. He stands in front of me as he tucks the shirt into the top of his pants, buttons his fly, and redoes his belt. "What do you want to do?" he asks as he buttons his shirt.

"I thought we were going to that party."

Finn shrugs. "Honestly, Emma and I don't get along. Her parents are super wealthy and have that conservative, old-fashioned mindset. She kind of has it too. We can if you want, but you didn't really seem to enjoy that other party. It'll be just more of the same, really."

"Well, what do you usually do on a Friday?"

He pulls out his cell phone and checks the time. "Ever been to the lighthouse? Down at Cape May?"

"Years ago," I say. With my dad, I almost add. "When I was a kid."

"Great, you can see if it's like you remember," he says.

Chapter 5

Finn's car is messy. The outside is covered with a fine layer of sand, and tiny patches of rust run along the edges of the doors on both sides. On top sits a rack to hold surfboards, which looks pretty new compared to the car. The backseat is filled with towels, sandals, a wetsuit, and a pair of board shorts. On the passenger seat are crumpled-up fast food bags, which Finn quickly gathers up and tosses into a trash can where he parked. "Sorry," he says hurriedly as he tidies things up, "I guess since I'm usually the only one in my car, I kind of let it get out of control."

"So, it's yours?"

"Yeah, all mine." He pats the dashboard. "I started saving money about a year after I got into surfing, the summer after my freshman year. My parents weren't always willing to drop me off and pick me up when I wanted to hit the beach. Kind of bummed me out. The day after I got my license, my dad went with me to the used car lot on the mainland. My parents helped me buy it and pay half the insurance. I cover gas and little repairs and such. It's worth it, though, to just be able to put my board on and be surfing like twenty minutes later. I mean, if I just surfed in Stone Harbor, I can always walk it from my place. But it's nice sometimes to check out other spots. Plus, for things like this—spur of the moment trips and stuff."

"That's cool." Then I add, "Must be nice."

"So, you have to share the car with your parents? I must

be spoiled, because I can't even imagine how that works. But I guess it's different in Chicago."

"I can't imagine what it would have been like dealing with two cars where we live. Having one was bad enough, like trying to find places to park, or needing to dig out a spot somewhere after it snowed. Plus, I can get around to school and cross-country practice on buses or the El."

"Was?" Finn asks.

As soon as he asks, I curse myself for not being more careful. Now I have to explain what happened to the car. Which will mean I have to explain the accident, and after that there is no way to avoid talking about Dad. It won't be the first time I've had to tell the story, but I've only hung out with Finn twice now, and it seems a little early.

"It was totaled. In an accident. I guess we just haven't gotten around to getting a new one yet."

"Was it bad? The accident?" Finn prods.

When I don't answer immediately, he glances quickly at me. I kind of nod yes and hope that's enough, but after the silence that follows, I decide its better if I just get it over with.

"My dad—he died. Like before they could even get him to the hospital. I broke my arm and leg and had to have surgery to pin both back together." I stop for a second, then add, "So yeah, I guess it was bad."

Finn simply responds, "I'm so sorry." I silently brace myself for the barrage of questions that always come next, about how the accident happened, and how long did it take for me to heal and are Mom and I okay now.

Instead, Finn says, "Hey, you're not hungry, are you? The last time I ate was before my shift started at two o'clock, and now I'm famished." He pulls into a parking lot for Wawa's, the local convenience store. He turns off the car and spins to grab his backpack from the backseat. As he ruffles through it to get his wallet he says, "If not, then you can wait here. I won't be long." I shake my head.

Then he's gone, and I'm left alone, not having to talk more about the accident. Which feels good.

We head to the Cape May Lighthouse, and Finn drives to the far northeast corner that looks directly over an inlet pond called Bunker Pond. He parks across from an observation deck for the wetlands here. Finn grabs his food and drink, and as he opens his door says, "The observation deck is pretty cool, but it's too dark to really see anything now. We should head down to the beach."

As Finn pulled into the parking lot and drove slowly toward the deck, my palms started sweating and my stomach clenched up. The bird sanctuary and observation deck were Dad's favorite places at Cape May. We didn't come every year, but whenever we did, he insisted we take a walk along the trails that went around the pond. I panic at the thought that Finn would want to walk one of the paths or hang out on the deck. I figured eventually I would end up walking the trails, but I didn't think it would be tonight. Before getting out of the car and following Finn, I let out a tiny sigh of relief. And hope he didn't notice I was slightly freaking out.

The ruins of a bunker built during World War II sit about a hundred yards down the beach. Finn heads right toward them at a brisk walk as soon as we exit the path through the dune. We climb on top and sit facing the ocean. He screws off the top of his ginger ale and takes a sip. "So, is it like you remember?"

"Yeah, sure," I shrug. "Actually, we spent most of our time walking the trails around the pond."

Finn launches into a story about how the first time he surfed was here on a school trip in junior high. "Wasn't really into any other sports before that. But now I'm hooked." He unwraps his sandwich and just before he takes a bite asks, "So, what about you? Why do you run?"

"Because it's when I can actually feel the best."

"Feel what? You mean like happy or something?"

"No, not that." I shake my head and think for a second. "I mean, really feel things. It makes whatever emotion you have at the moment stronger: happiness, sadness, contentment. It really is just a way of feeling more."

Finn gives a nod and shoots me a smile.

Just after midnight, I decide I should call Liam. We have a one a.m. curfew while at the beach house. Mom and Aunt Marion have this idyllic notion of Stone Harbor and still think it's the quaint and safe town it was when they were little, so they give us some leeway. They are not completely wrong. It's definitely safer than Chicago or Baltimore. Last year, Liam and I stayed up all night on the beach to watch the sunrise. We drank Mountain Dew and ate gummy bears to stay awake. Dad joined us just before daybreak. But that was different—everyone knew where we would be, unlike tonight. So, I know we shouldn't push it that much.

"I should find out where those two are," I say. As I call Liam's cell, Finn just sits quietly and stares off into the dark waters. Liam's phone rings and rings, and I'm about ready to hang up and text him when he answers. I can barely hear him over the loud music and laughing in the background.

"Melissa and I are about to head home," he says. "We had to drive to Emma's party. Can you meet us somewhere on the boardwalk? Where are you?"

"Cape May. At the lighthouse."

"Dude," Liam shouts over the background noise. "That's

thirty minutes away. In the wrong direction! We'll never make it."

I put my hand over the phone and say, "Liam and Melissa are still at Emma's. They can't come get me and get back before our curfew. Do you think you can get me at least back to Stone Harbor by one o'clock?"

"Happy to do it," he says. "If we leave now, you'll have time to spare."

"Look, I think Finn can get me home," I say to Liam, but it's gotten so loud I can barely hear him. "Liam?" I yell again. He's saying something about needing to leave now, but then I can't hear him. Finally, I just hang up. As Finn and I walk toward his car, I text Liam, "Finn will get me home. I'll see you at the house."

"Perfect," Liam texts back.

As badly as I wanted to not spend the evening with Melissa, I'm angry that Liam essentially left me on my own. During the ride back, I thank Finn about five times for driving me all the way back to Stone Harbor.

He smiles and says, "No problem. That's where I live, remember?"

When Finn drops me off, I notice that Aunt Marion's car is not in the driveway. I quietly climb upstairs to Liam's and my room. There are two bedrooms on the third floor, but just out of tradition, Liam and I share the largest one that overlooks the front of the house and has a view of the beach. I sit on the edge of my bed and stare at Liam's unmade, messy one. For some reason I make it for him. I brush my teeth and pull off my clothes before climbing into bed. I glance at my phone; it's 12:48 a.m. I text Liam, "I'm here. You still have twelve minutes." I fall asleep before I even know if he texts me back.

When I wake up the next morning, Liam is sleeping in his bed with his clothes on. I check my phone, and he never even responded to my last text. I can only guess he got in by one a.m., or just a bit after.

I creep downstairs so as to not wake up Mom and Aunt Marion. As I step into the family room, I'm brought back to the mornings after I would run and Dad would make pancakes. I close my eyes. I can almost hear him whisking the batter in one of the metal bowls, humming something indiscernible to himself. I can see myself cooling down and doing stretches on the floor, my stomach grumbling as I wait for Dad to tiptoe into the family room and whisper, "Come on. They're ready."

I walk out onto the porch. The sun has yet to come up over the ocean, but it's getting lighter every minute. I know the beach will be empty for another thirty minutes. That's where I want to be when the sun comes up.

Dad's old thermos is in the kitchen, and I fill it with water before I leave. When I get to the beach, I open the thermos and inhale. It has a strange smell of old coffee and detergent, but both are weak and ephemeral. I close my eyes and try to remember what Dad looked like on these early mornings, his eyes closed, steam wafting out of his thermos into his face. I wish I had asked him what he was smelling. Was it just the scent of the coffee? What had I missed all those years? I can still see his face, his hollow cheeks, his tired eyes and graying hair, but like the smells from his thermos the details are fuzzy. He is still in my memory—but only almost.

Despite his busy schedule, he came to almost all my races. When I started cross-country, he started studying the sport. He read the biography of Steve Prefontaine and tracked the rosters of the teams my school raced against. We always talked about my strategy, my goal, and how to approach my races together.

"You're a pacer," Dad would tell me. "Just keep the guy you want to beat a little ahead of you. Let him set the pace, and you keep your energy. Then sprint him down at the finish line." Having Dad there made me feel comfortable.

Now, as I stand on the beach, I'm afraid I might forever lose how it feels to be with Dad. My mouth is dry, and a lump hangs in my throat, making it hard to swallow. There's a sun-bleached log near the dunes, and I walk over to it. I kick off my flip-flops and put the thermos down next to them. It's still chilly, but I take off my hooded sweatshirt and ball it up because I don't want it to get gross and sweaty. Then I take off along the beach, running with the water on my right, the waves splashing up my ankles and shins. I close my eyes and try to feel like it was with Dad. Or to at least feel anything.

I run for three miles. The seagulls circle around me, crying as I run, diving into the water. My legs feel heavy and slow, my heart races and my lungs explode. I struggle more in these three miles than I ever have before. I feel slow and heavy. I've lost ten pounds since the accident but most of my clothes still fit. I guess it was all muscle.

I get back to my flip-flops, sweatshirt, and Dad's thermos. I sit down on the log, panting. Tears well up in my eyes and spill down my cheeks, mixing with the sweat that has gathered on my face. I roll my head back, letting the sun and wind dry my face as I catch my breath. I close my eyes and try to remember Dad. I smell the thermos, trying to remember his hot chocolate. Or his pancakes. Instead, I only cry harder.

Then I feel stupid. What must I look like, a seventeen-year-old boy, practically an adult, sitting on the beach crying? I look off to my right and see an old couple holding hands and walking a dog. We are the only people on the beach. As they get closer, I wipe my face with my sweatshirt so it won't look like I was crying. But before they get too close, they stop to throw sticks into the waves, and their dog runs after them. I watch them for a bit, but the sweat is starting to evaporate and it leaves a chill on my skin. Eventually, I walk to the beach house.

When I get back, Mom is sitting at the kitchen table in her bathrobe. She holds a steaming cup of coffee, and she seems to be staring at nothing. Despite it being early, she looks exhausted. Like Liam, she has green eyes, but hers are dark, more forest-green. Swollen, puffy bags hang underneath them. Before Dad died, she always wore her hair over her shoulders, and it was bronze and shiny. Now it has gray streaks and is pulled into a bun. It is pulled tightly around the edges of her round face, making it seem even rounder. She doesn't hear me come in, and I stand in the doorway, realizing how little we have seen of each other since Aunt Marion and Liam arrived. Finally, I walk into the kitchen.

"Hi sweetie." She smiles as I slide into my seat.

"Hi Mom."

"Where are you coming from?" she asks. I put Dad's thermos on the table. "Did you go to the beach to run?"

I think about it for a second. I had not gone to the beach to run, but that's exactly what I ended up doing. But I didn't want to say so. I know there will be a thousand questions. How did it feel? Did it make me happier? Did it remind of me of Dad?

Or she might not ask me anything at all, which might be worse.

"No," I shake my head, although I'm sure she knows the true answer. My hair is mussed up and sand is spattered up the back of my shirt. "You're up early," I say. "Are you hungry? Maybe we can make pancakes?" I regret saying that as soon as the words left my mouth.

Mom picks up her coffee cup, and before taking a sip, she says, "No thanks, dear. I'm not much of a breakfast person."

Then we both just sit there in silence.

Chapter 6

The next weekend as we're eating dinner, Liam says, "I saw a sign for a local band playing at a club next to the movie theatre downtown. I thought we could check it out."

"At a club?" Aunt Marion asks. "How are you going to get into a club?"

"It's an eighteen-and-under place, Mom," Liam sighs. He looks at me. "It's only five bucks to get in, so even if they're bad, I figure no big loss."

I don't answer immediately. Ever since the day he left me with Finn at the shooting gallery, Liam has come up with something for us to do after dinner, and we just happen to run into Melissa and Finn. The first time it happened, Liam said he really wanted to see a movie that was playing down at the theater. When we entered the lobby, I went straight to the ticket counter, but Liam grabbed my arm and said, "Hey, look who's here." Melissa and Finn were standing at the concession stand.

Melissa did that jump-clap-laugh thing that I'm starting to hate. "Why are you guys here?" she asked.

I almost laughed at how ridiculous her question was and how obvious it was they'd planned this. Liam and Melissa immediately started talking about their favorite movie candy. Finn walked up to me and whispered, "How stupid do they think we are?"

I shrugged. "I should have figured it out when Liam said he really wanted to see this movie." It was some popular romantic comedy starring some guy from a band trying to become an actor. When he suggested it, I figured he was just bored and wanted to get out of the house. "Neither of us listen to the guy's band, and Liam really can't stand rom-coms," I added.

"Melissa loves them. She drags me to a couple of them every summer."

"Lucky you." I laughed.

"And now you too," he sighed.

We found four seats together, but Liam and Melissa sat in the middle, with Finn and me on the ends. I fell asleep halfway through.

So when we get to the club and Melissa and Finn are standing outside, it's not surprising. Liam and Melissa are done pretending we just all happened to show up at the same place because Melissa says to Liam, "I got you a ticket, and Finn bought one for Tyler."

Finn hands me a ticket. I dig in my wallet and only have a ten-dollar bill.

"I don't have change," Finn says. "Just keep it."

I shake my head. "You didn't have to do that." I hold out the ten-dollar bill for him to take. "You can pay me back later."

Finn stands there for a second. "No, really, I wanted to," he says. As soon as he says it, I feel awkward. It's obvious he does too, because he sheepishly puts his hands in his pocket and looks away. Liam and Melissa are staring at the two of us, and I'm still holding my money out toward Finn.

"Jesus, you two," Liam says as he grabs the bill from me, yanks Finn's hand out of his pocket, and jams it into his palm. "You can buy Tyler a drink when we get in. Let's just go."

We stand in line to get in, and as we hand over our tickets the bouncer checks our IDs. He has two boxes of wristbands, pink and green. All four of us get pink, and Finn turns to me and says, "We're all under twenty-one."

Turns out Liam's eighteen-and-under statement to Aunt Marion was a lie, but I'm not surprised. None of us say a word as we wander to an empty spot in front of the stage, and then Finn and Liam go off to get us drinks. There's no music yet. It's actually quiet enough that we could talk, but Melissa is on her phone the entire time, looking at pictures and texting.

About ten minutes later, Finn and Liam return with four big red cups. After Finn hands me my drink, I take a sip. It's beer, not soda.

I give Liam a sidewise glance. "You got beer?"

"Finn knew the bartender and hooked us up." Liam takes another sip. I look at my cup, but when I don't take another sip, Liam asks, "Is that okay? Do you want me to go get something else?"

I shrug. "No. It doesn't matter."

"Seriously," Liam says and grabs my drink. "I can get you a soda."

"I said it's fine," I snap, and take my cup back. We just stare at each other. This is getting more common, these awkward moments between us. Moments when something needs to be said but I'm not quite sure what. And neither does he. Liam gives a little scowl.

Melissa is standing next to Liam and taps his shoulder to show him a picture on her phone. "Look," she says. "Emma's puppy. So adorbs!"

I stare at the stage. Nothing happens. It's 9:07 and the band was supposed to go on at nine. Melissa continues to show Liam cute dog pictures. I look over and Finn is talking to a guy and a girl. I can't hear what they are saying, but the guy is telling some story and Finn and the girl are laughing. Finn takes a sip of his drink, then turns his head just slightly and catches me looking. He winks, gives me a smile, and turns back to the conversation. I look down at my beer and wonder if I would have been better off staying home.

The room slowly fills up, and by 9:17 three guys come out on the stage. Some of the crowd starts to cheer, but one of the guys on the stage waves his arms and shakes his head, indicating they're not the band. The three of them start hooking up the speakers and soundboard. After another ten minutes, the band finally saunters onto the stage. There are two guys and two girls. One guy is the lead singer and the other the drummer while the girls play bass and lead guitar. When they come out on stage, the bass player saunters up to the mic and yells, "We are Transient! One, two, three, go!"

They play mostly covers, but the bass player sings lead on two original songs that sound pretty decent. Liam and Melissa dance with each other and talk, but it's too loud for me to hear what they say. When they're tired of that, Melissa pulls out her phone and Liam stares over her shoulder as she scrolls through more pictures, probably cute puppies or something else just as annoying. Liam goes back to get them more drinks at least twice.

Finn comes and stands next to me, but it's too loud to say anything. I've had maybe three sips of my beer, and during one of the songs, Finn takes the cup from my hand, walks over to the shelf along the wall, and puts his empty cup and my full one down. He comes back and smiles at me. I nod.

"You've been a wonderful crowd," the singer yells, "and we love you."

A couple of people in the audience yell back, "We love you!"

The female bassist steps up to the microphone and says, "Thanks for coming out tonight! Here is one last song."

The drummer counts out four beats using his drumsticks and they launch into a cover of a song that was popular about three years ago. I had this song on my playlist when I started cross-county, and hearing it makes me think of running along Lake Michigan back home. Which makes me think of Dad. Which makes a lump appear in my throat, and my heart start to race. I make a dash to the bathroom and lock myself in a stall. As soon as the door is closed, the tears run down my cheeks.

I pull my legs up so no one can see me. I just sit in the stall, wishing I had never come out tonight. Or maybe even come to Stone Harbor this summer. I wonder if this is how the rest of my life is going to be—that no matter where I am, I just won't want to be there.

After I was released from the hospital, it was about another week before Dad's funeral. There were days when I thought it couldn't come soon enough. For some reason, going to the funeral meant I was going to see Dad again, one last time. I had been having nightmares about the accident. Ones where Dad always knew he was going to die and that it scared him. I wanted to hear him tell me he wasn't scared and he is fine now. I know it sounds crazy, but I had gone over the conversation in my head for days before the funeral.

"Does it hurt?" I would start.

"No. I'm fine. You don't need to worry."

"Were you scared?"

"I was only scared for you."

"Don't be. The doctors say I'll heal just fine."

"I love you," he would say.

"I love you too," I would answer back, because I never got one last chance to say it.

When I got into the funeral parlor and saw Dad lying there in the casket, I froze. I stood in the doorway of the room and wouldn't go in. I didn't want to see him, didn't want to be there, didn't want anything to do with any of it. Finally, Mom asked if I wanted her to go with me to see him, but I said no. I was still using crutches, so she asked one of the funeral parlor attendants to get me a folding chair and put it next to Dad so I could sit.

For the longest time, I sat there by myself and realized how wrong I was. There were no answers. He wasn't okay, it probably did hurt, and I'm sure he was scared as hell when it happened. This wasn't my last chance to be with him. He was gone. It was just his body dressed in a suit I'd never seen him wear before.

And I couldn't handle any of that.

Just like tonight. I can't handle being here, despite the fact that the band is actually pretty good. Everyone out there is laughing and dancing and having a good time. Except for me. I've locked myself in a stall because of a stupid song. I stay in the bathroom until the band finishes and I hear Liam call out, "Tyler, you in here?"

I quickly wipe my face with my sleeve, blow my nose with some toilet paper, and then flush it down the toilet. I wait just a second before I come out and head straight to the sink.

"Dude, you okay?" Liam comes up to me.

"Yeah, fine," I say, but my nose is running so I sniff.

"You sure? Do you need me to take you home or something?"

"I'm fine," I say, still washing my hands. "Just had to use the bathroom, that's all." I turn off the water and walk over to the towels to dry my hands. "So, what's next?"

But I know damn well what is next. Melissa and Liam will take off. Melissa always has some other place she needs to be, like she promised Emma she would meet her later, or her parents have gone to Atlantic City and since no one is home to take out the dog she has to leave. She'll get Liam to take her. That is what always happens.

Liam looks at me funny. "I dunno. Is there something you want to do? You come up with an idea and I'm all for it."

I shake my head and say, "Let's go see what Finn and Melissa are up to."

"Okay. Let's go," he says. But we don't leave. We stand there staring each other down until Finn walks in. He unzips his fly as he walks over to one of the urinals.

"There you two are," he says with his face toward the wall. "Melissa thought you left already, so she's out front looking for you." He finishes up and washes his hands at the sink. When neither Liam nor I say anything or move, he looks at both of us through the mirror and says, "Is everything okay?"

"Yeah," Liam says. "Tyler and I were just figuring out what to do next."

Finn shakes his hands dry, and then turns around and leans against the sink counter. "You and Tyler? Melissa said she already made plans for you and her to meet Emma and her boyfriend at the coffee shop for some dessert."

I cross my arms and lean back on the counter next to Finn. This is exactly what I had expected. I'm pissed and want to let Liam have it, but I can't with Finn here. Instead, I glare at Liam and say, "What Liam meant was that he was trying to help me figure out what I should do because he's going with Melissa."

Liam glares at me. "Look," he starts, but before he can finish, both his and Finn's phones buzz with messages. Liam doesn't react but Finn fishes his phone out of his pocket. "It's Melissa.

She's freaking out because she can't find anyone." Another text arrives. "And you're going to be late to meet Emma." Then a third comes. "And she doesn't find it funny that we've left her alone out there." He puts his phone away and laughs. "Well, she probably won't want to come join us in here." But his smirk quickly fades when he realizes that neither Liam nor I laughed. And that we are still pretty much just staring each other down.

"No," Liam says dryly. "Probably not. Guess now that you two have found each other, you can figure out what you want to do. Have fun." He leaves the bathroom.

"Wow," Finn says. "That was . . . weird. Is he okay?"

"Yeah, he's fine." I sigh and stand up straight. "Come on, let's go find something to do." We head out of the club and up the street toward downtown Stone Harbor.

Finn is right. This is weird. Not what just happened tonight, but what has been happening all summer. It's obvious Melissa and Liam want to spend time together, and I get it. But I also get the sense that Liam is trying to force Finn and I to hang out more. Maybe it's a way to not feel guilty for ditching me all the time.

To be honest, it's not being ditched that bothers me but what it does to me. Losing Liam every night we go out makes me feel alone, repeatedly. It feels like I'm a burden to him, or that he can't stand being with me anymore. As soon as it happens, I'm devastated.

But then, after the initial hurt, I'm fine because Finn is always there with some plan in mind: a taco stand on the north end of the island, a local ice cream shop that makes the best malts, or just the default trip to Cape May. And I go along with it because it works.

But tonight, I can't get over it. It felt like Liam and I were finally going to get this all out in the open. Then it never happened.

"So, which will it be?" Finn says, breaking my train of thought.

"What?"

He rolls his eyes. "Sometimes I don't think you want me here. You definitely don't listen to half of what I say."

I'm not sure how to answer that, so I don't. I just smile, hopefully one that says I'm sorry.

Finn sighs. "I said it's only a short walk to my house, and we could get my car. Then we could head down to the Cape May Lighthouse or hit up Wildwood again. Or, we could just find something to do here in Stone Harbor. What do you think?"

We have been to the Cape May Lighthouse three times over the past two weeks, each time Melissa and Liam have ditched us. Is that going to be the rest of my summer here at the beach? Evenings at the lighthouse with Finn? At first, I think that sounds horrible, but then I realize maybe not. It might not be what I thought this summer would be like, but it isn't as bad as I thought. I suddenly have a mental image of me hanging with Finn next year when we come, not Liam. And strangely, I'm fine with that.

As I'm contemplating all this, my stomach grumbles loud enough that Finn can hear it, and we both kind of giggle.

"Good idea. Let's find something to eat. Anything in particular?"

I shrug, and then say, "Let's find some pizza."

"That is one thing Stone Harbor doesn't have a shortage of," he says.

As we walk back toward the middle of downtown, Finn

looks up pizza places on his phone. He is not joking. About ten places all within two blocks of downtown show up. A couple are Italian restaurants that include pizza on the menu.

"Too stuffy," Finn says as he reads through the places. Then he finds a place that is named Pizza Open. Despite all the years I've been coming to Stone Harbor, I've never heard of it.

"Actually," he says, showing me pictures of it on his phone, "I don't go there very often because it's only open during the summer when the tourists are here. But you can buy lots of different pizzas by the slice. It's kind of hard to find, to tell the truth, because it's across the courtyard behind the arcade. It has a good crowd. Let's go there."

"You're the expert," I say, and we head off.

We both order two slices and a drink, then sit in the courtyard. As we're eating, the guy and the girl from the concert Finn was talking to come over and join us. They are in the same class as Finn, and he introduces us. They chat about local gossip— who's going out with whom, did Finn hear the gym teacher is finally retiring? I don't say much, but Finn definitely makes an effort to let me know he hasn't forgotten I'm there. Mostly, he just gives me a sidewise glance or quick smile. I smile back.

At a quarter to one, I say I have to get home.

"Same with me," Finn says, and we toss our trash into the wastebasket and return our plastic plates to Pizza Open, which ironically is now closed. Finn and I head down Main Street to Second Avenue, which is the street our beach house is on. I start to head north toward home, and Finn comes with me.

"Where are you going?" I ask.

Finn stutters, "I was . . . walking you home, I guess."

I stop. "That's not necessary," I say. "I've been doing this since I was like, twelve. It's just four blocks. You don't have to go out of your way." As I say that, I realize I don't know exactly where he lives. I quickly add, "I mean, unless it is on your way."

"No," Finn says. "I live that way." He motions with his head up Main Street toward the bay. "I just thought . . ." and he stops there.

It's awkward for a moment, so I quickly say, "That's crazy. It's late, so you can just go home. I'm sure I'll see you tomorrow. Or sometime soon."

"Yeah, okay." Finn shoves his hands in his pockets. Neither of us says anything. Then he spins on his heels and heads back up Main Street toward his house. I turn and head home.

The first floor of the beach house is dark, and I quietly make my way to the third floor. As expected, Liam isn't home. I brush my teeth, wash my face, and then strip off my clothes and drop into bed.

I dream about buying running shoes with Dad. He keeps bringing me different pairs to try on and asking me which ones I like.

"But what if I don't want to run anymore?"

"Then don't," Dad says, and slips a pair of shoes on my feet. "How do these feel?"

I shrug. "Like running shoes," I say. I look at them, not sure why he brought them out. "How do they look?"

I'm still looking at the shoes when Dad says, "You can't ask me that anymore. We'd better find someone else."

I look up and Finn is in the store looking at surfing boards along the wall. Liam is with him, helping him pick out a new one. I look back down, but Dad is gone.

Chapter 7

Three days later I wake up to heavy drops being driven against the small window in our room. As I stretch, I look over and see that Liam has a pillow over his head. Once again, I got home before he did. Last night Liam and I met Melissa and Finn on the mainland for Chinese. Then Melissa announces she and Liam are meeting Emma and her boyfriend for movie. Liam asked if Finn and I wanted to join, but it felt too much like a double-date to me, making us interlopers. Finn said he knew a cool skate park with lights, and we hung out there watching other kids skate until about midnight. What time Liam got back, I don't know. And quite frankly, I don't care anymore.

After I go to the bathroom and splash some water on my face, I walk down to the family room. It's empty again, and I suddenly remember a rainy day like this when Dad and I each did a crossword from old issues of the Tribune he had brought with him from work. I can hear the scratching of our pencils on the paper as we asked each other clues.

"Five letters, what comes after phi, chi, and psi?" I asked. "Second letter is m."

Without even looking up from his puzzle, Dad said, "It's Greek. Omega. It means 'great O.'"

I shrugged, and then wrote it in.

"High school class that is not PG," Dad mused. "Five letters."

I laughed. Then looking out of the corner of my eyes, I whispered, "Sex Ed?"

Dad folded his paper on his lap and shook his head. "Right," he said, "Right." Then he scribbled in the letters.

Dad insisted we not have a TV or radio here. "At the beach house, we connect," he would say. But we always had magazines and newspapers. Now a couple of old Economists are scattered on the end tables, but that's it. I'm surprised Aunt Marion hasn't thrown them away yet.

I decide I need to do a crossword, so I head outside and down to the Wawa at the end of the block. Because it reminds me a little of Dad, I buy a latte and a chocolate muffin to eat as I walk back home. As I pull off my raincoat and stomp my feet dry at the door of the beach house, Liam comes down the stairs. He is still in his boxers and a T-shirt.

"Hey," I say. He only nods back, still not awake, and shuffles into the kitchen.

I walk to the couch and pull the newspaper I bought out from under my arm. The Wawa only carried USA Today and the New York Times. Dad often called USA Today "the little paper that tried," so I bought the Times. As I sit on the couch, Liam comes back in with a glass of orange juice and a piece of bread with jam on it. He sits on the other end of the couch, points to the paper on my lap and asks, "What's that?"

"A newspaper."

"I know that. But why do you have one?"

"For the crossword puzzle."

"You do the crossword?"

"Yeah. I mean, why not. Don't you?"

"No way." Liam shakes his head and takes a bite of his bread. He pulls out his phone, and I get to work on the puzzle. And I realize this is okay. This works. Me doing crosswords and remembering Dad, and Liam doing . . . whatever it is he's doing on his phone. This feels okay to me. This I can do for the entire summer. I mean, the other night I was trying to convince myself I did not need Liam. I could make do without him because Finn always had some plan to fill my time. But it's moments like this when I realize that Liam and I are still good. Maybe if we can just focus on ourselves, then the two of us will be okay. Without Melissa, without Finn, we're back to normal. Kind of.

I'm halfway through the puzzle when I hear the kitchen door open. Aunt Marion hobbles into the family room carrying a small TV. "Liam, help me. I'm about to drop this," she huffs.

Liam jumps up and the two of them carry the TV to the foot of the fireplace and put it on the ground. Mom is carrying what looks like an old game console. The cables are all wound around her arms, and it takes her a few minutes to disentangle herself.

"What's this?" I ask as the three of them start to set everything up.

"I found them at the flea market for fifty dollars," Aunt Marion says. "Not bad, right?"

"But why?"

The three of them stop what they're doing and look at me.

"I just thought you two would like it." Aunt Marion shrugs. "Something to do on rainy days. Like today. I know it's old, but still." She wipes some dust of the top of the TV.

"But why?" I say again. "We don't need them. We've never had a TV or a PlayStation—"

"It's a Nintendo." Liam cuts me off. "I think it's cool. We can play Mario Kart or something retro like that."

I pause, searching for how to say what I am thinking. It's like they forgot the rule. Dad's rule. Here we connect. But not anymore. Not this summer, I guess.

"Whatever," I say and make a point of putting all my attention toward my crossword puzzle. After no one says anything for about a minute, Liam rubs his face and says, "I'm going to take a shower." Then he goes up the stairs. Aunt Marion never says anything, just heads into the kitchen. I can hear her grinding coffee beans.

Mom sits down next to me on the couch. I purposely avoid looking at her. But I can't do the crossword either because I have tears in my eyes. We sit for a few minutes until Mom says, "Are you okay? If not, we can take it back." She runs her hand through my hair.

"Why bother?" I whisper, hoping my voice won't break. "It's just a TV."

But we both know it is more than that.

Later, the storm clouds finally pass and the sun comes out to make the day wet, heavy, and humid. Liam and I walk downtown to check out what new movies have arrived, and maybe see one. On the way there, he calls Melissa on his cell phone to see if she wants to join us. After asking her, there is a long silence. He puts his hand over his phone and says, "She's at the boardwalk in Wildwood and wants to know if we want to come down there."

"Well, what about the movies?" I ask. "Don't you want to see one? It was your idea."

"Really, I don't care what we do. I just wanted to get out of the house."

"Fine," I say. He gets back on the phone and tells her we are coming to Wildwood. There is another long pause, then he hangs up the phone. "She said Finn can meet her there, and once we are all together we can figure out what to do."

I don't respond because there's no need for me to say anything. Since the night of the band, there's been this uncomfortable strain between Liam and me. Sometimes we're fine, like this morning with the crossword, before the arrival of the TV. But other times, it goes from being a merely uncomfortable moment to this oppressive expectation. Like we're supposed to be all happy and excited to just be with each other, but we're not. Recently, Liam sometimes sleeps in the spare room by himself. It felt okay that first night, going to sleep in the room alone. But when I woke up the next morning and saw his empty bed, I resented him for it. I felt really abandoned by him. But some days, just getting up in the morning and having him there in the room with me has started to bother me too. To be honest, sitting in silence in a dark movie theater was about all I could stand doing with Liam today. But I'm not too worried, because I know that the day will end with Liam and Melissa off doing something and Finn and I doing the same. I'm actually really fine with that.

We don't say a word the entire way back. Liam stops a couple of times because he keeps getting texts. He doesn't say so, but I know they're from Melissa. By the time I reach the beach house, Liam is still walking up the sidewalk. Aunt Marion is sitting on the porch reading, and as I come up the steps, she asks about the movie.

"We decided to go to Wildwood instead, to spend time with Liam's girlfriend, Melissa," I say without stopping. "We're going to take Mom's car."

I head into the house to find the keys in the kitchen. As I'm rummaging through Mom's purse, I hear Liam coming up the porch steps. Aunt Marion and Liam talk on the porch, but I can't make out what they are saying. I know Liam hasn't said anything about Melissa to Aunt Marion yet, and just mentioning some strange girl's name—let alone calling her his girlfriend—would cause her to quiz him ruthlessly. Liam has this thing about 'meeting the girlfriend,' and so he usually never mentions them to his parents. Which only makes Aunt Marion suspicious and try to pry even more. It was a mean thing to do, but I'm angry about this whole situation and how he lets Melissa change up everything.

I find the keys in Mom's purse and grab a handful of pretzels before heading back out to the porch. Aunt Marion and Liam aren't saying anything, but the strain in the air lets me know my girlfriend comment stirred things up. Liam is leaning against the railing, his arms folded tightly across his chest. Aunt Marion has her book in her lap and is staring intently at Liam. I lean against the door and toss a couple of pretzels in my mouth. I want to watch what comes next.

"Well," Aunt Marion finally says, "Since your mom and I haven't met this new friend that Liam says you both have"— she stresses the word both, and I guess Liam has been arguing that Melissa's not his girlfriend—"I've decided you should have her over for dinner this Saturday."

"Great." I smile. "Melissa will be thrilled, I'm sure." Aunt Marion eyes me suspiciously, then picks up her book and says, "Tell her to come at six, Liam. And not to be late."

To say the car ride to Wildwood is uncomfortable is an understatement. Since we've left the porch, Liam and I have not said a word to each other. Liam has his phone out and is engaged in a seemingly intense conversation with Melissa. He's probably telling her about the little stunt I just pulled. I should feel guilty, but strangely I don't. We hit the drawbridge that will take us onto Wildwood Avenue, but a fishing boat is moving in from the ocean, so we sit. I connect my phone to the car's speakers to play some music while we wait. As I am jumping through songs, Liam dryly says, "Melissa doesn't know if Finn is coming or not, and she wants you to ask him." He gazes out the passenger side window.

"What?"

"She says she doesn't know where Finn is, or if he wants to come or not. She just figured you would know where he was or have talked to him or something, and we could all just go to lunch together."

"That's not what you told me on the way to the movie theater. You said she was meeting Finn already."

"I know, that's what I thought too. But when I asked again"— he holds up his phone to indicate that's what all the texting was about—"She said Finn can meet us. Meaning if you wanted to ask him. So, that's all I can say."

I don't say anything. None of this makes sense to me. Finally, the boat is gone, and the bridge is back down. I put the car in gear but keep my foot on the brake.

"Why do I have to call him? Why can't she?"

"Because she says . . . " Liam hesitates, then starts again. "I mean, he's your—" A car behind us honks, cutting him off. I stomp on the gas pedal, lurching us onto the draw-bridge.

"Well, it doesn't matter why," I bark. "I can't. I don't have his number. And I'm sure he doesn't have mine. Hasn't it occurred to either of you that Finn and I have never called each other? We never make plans. You two do. I see Finn only because, as far as I can tell, she drags him with her whenever you two make plans."

Liam doesn't say anything. What can he say? He knows I'm right, and anything he might offer will only make me more pissed. "Look," I continue, "this was her idea. Tell her she needs to find him. Not me."

Liam texts her as we continue across the drawbridge. We drive into Wildwood, find a parking spot, and sit. After two more exchanges with Melissa, Liam puts his phone away and climbs out of the car. Before he closes the door he leans back in and says to me, "We should meet her at the shooting gallery."

It takes us ten minutes to walk to the shooting gallery, and when we arrive, Finn and Melissa are talking to each other. Finn is wearing his work vest and shirt. He's standing outside of the gallery and a college-aged girl in a matching uniform is working behind him. As Liam and I approach, Melissa and Finn stop talking.

"So," Melissa says to Liam, "Finn wants to go to swimming."

"Actually, I wanted to go surfing," Finn says to Melissa, but then forces a smile at Liam and me when he says, "but since we all can't do that, we should go swimming instead."

Once I hear Finn's comment, I have to struggle to not scream in frustration. It is so obvious that Melissa had no clue what Finn was up to. It's so stupid, her wanting me to have to invite him. I'm about to lay into her for the mess she's made, but she's not evening paying attention. She's reading a message on her cell phone.

I take a deep breath to calm myself down, and then finally say, "That doesn't work either. Liam and I didn't bring our swimming suits."

"We should hurry up and think of something," Melissa says without looking up from her phone, "because I agreed to meet Emma for lunch in an hour."

I can tell by the look on Finn and Liam's faces that this is news to them. No one says anything. Finn throws his hands in the air as he laughs. Liam drags his hand down his face, gathering his cool.

"Look," Liam says with his hands still covering part of his face. "An hour is not enough to do anything, really. Finn, you, wanted to go surfing, so go. The three of us can walk around or something before meeting Emma for lunch."

I'm not cool with that. That last thing I want to do right now is spend any amount of time with Liam and Melissa. The look on Melissa's face pretty much says the same thing.

"Or," Liam continues, "if you don't want to have lunch with us, Tyler, I can take you back to Stone Harbor, and then Melissa and I can meet Emma."

"Fine," I say, somewhat relieved that I won't have to spend the afternoon with the two of them. I'm not sure what I will do once I get to Stone Harbor, but that will be easier to handle than the alternative.

"Actually, my shift is over, so why don't you two just go find Emma now, and I can take Tyler home," Finn says. "I can surf somewhere in Stone Harbor after I drop him off."

No one objects, because it's the best solution. We all just stand there for a second. Then Melissa says, "I guess we will just have to plan on us all having lunch or something together later this week."

I just shake my head, because I can't believe she really thinks the four of us doing anything together after this fiasco is a good idea. But then Liam does something that blows my mind even more.

"Actually, we will. Tyler and I are supposed to invite both of you to dinner at our place on Saturday. A kind of meet-the-parents thing."

Melissa's eyes widen, and she does that jumping-and-clapping thing I hate so much. Finn shoots me that smile of his, but I'm kind of dumbstruck so don't react. He furrows his brow, so I quickly blurt out to reassure him, "Yeah. It will be fun. I can't wait."

"Well," Liam claps his hands together. "I guess we can go find Emma and see if she wants to have lunch early." He extends his hand toward me, waiting for the car keys. At the same time he stares me down with a wicked smile that lets me know he just got me back for the stunt I pulled on the porch earlier. I don't follow how that works, so I just kind of shrug as I hand over the keys. Then Liam loops his arm into Melissa's and they head off toward the car.

"Again," Finn says once they are gone. "That was weird."

I nod, still dumbstruck.

Then Finn and I stand around awkwardly, the piano player pumping out ragtime.

Finally, he clears his throat and asks, "Do you surf?"

I only shake my head in reply.

"Because," Finn continues seamlessly, "I've got an extra board in my car, and I'm sure I can find an extra pair of shorts in there too. It's basically my gym locker during the summer."

Before I figure out how to kindly turn down his offer to take me surfing, he turns to the girl behind the stand and says he's leaving, and she waves from across the gallery. He disappears into the back for two minutes, and when he returns, his hat and vest are gone.

He pats my shoulder and says, "Come on, the tide waits for no one," and heads down the boardwalk. I wait for a moment. Then I follow him.

As a distance runner, your body is slim and light. Extra weight is just that, extra weight, and it slows you down if it isn't muscle. Runners are usually all leg, able to take long strides with little effort, saving their energy for the end of the race. I am built like a runner: thin arms and legs, but muscular. My chest and stomach are flat—not tiny, but without the bulk and extra muscle that a wrestler or a football player might have. My legs are strong and lean, especially my thighs. As I watch Finn remove his shirt and dig through his car, I realize that I, like all my friends on the cross-country team, am built to run. Unlike Finn, who is built, I imagine, to surf.

The first thing I notice is his skin. Where I am merely brown from spending only a few hours each day on the beach and in the sun, Finn is bronzed, as if the color runs to his bone, not just a layer of his skin. His chest and stomach look sculpted out of driftwood. His jeans hang loosely from his hips, partly because he unbuttoned them when he took off his shirt, and partly because his stomach and waist funnel smoothly into them. His shoulders and arms are taut and muscular from hours spent swimming through the waves, pulling his board out into the surf. His hair is bleached from a combination of the sun, the salt, and the repeated showering after coming in from the ocean. As he stands bent over with the top half of his body lost in the back of his car, I realize we could not have been built more differently.

"Okay," he says, pulling his head out of the back seat, "I only have one towel. But we're in luck, I do have two suits." In his hands he has two pairs of long board shorts. Both are patterned, one blue and the other red. "I think I'm probably a little bigger than you in the waist, so you can just use the tie string to keep them on. The blue ones are clean, and you can use the towel to change. I'll just hide behind the door."

I'm leaning against the back end of his car, and he tosses the towel and shorts to me. Before I can even catch them, he slips off his shoes and throws them in the back of the car. With a quick glance around, he pulls the car door tight against him and drops his jeans and underwear. He picks them up off the ground, balls them together, and tosses them into the abyss of his car. He grabs his shorts, which he had slung over the door before he started to strip and turns to look at me. He is completely naked, standing in the doorjamb holding his shorts, and I haven't even started.

Feeling suddenly self-conscious, I turn to face the car. The guys on my track team and I have seen each other naked hundreds of times, showering after practices, or doing quick changes in car doors at meets behind a school building, just like this. I've known them for years and it's never been a big deal.

But I only met Finn six weeks ago, and that first night I saw him partially naked when he changed out of his work clothes in the back of the shooting gallery. And now I'm seeing him completely naked. I notice the tan line that runs right above his crotch, and how white and pale his thighs are. Then I blush, because it dawns on me I'm just staring at him. I quickly wrap the towel around my waist and kick off my shoes. I lose my balance a little and instinctively grab the car door that's hiding Finn to steady myself.

"Nervous?" he asks.

I give him a quizzical look before I pull my shirt over my head.

"About the surfing." He continues. "I mean. I think you'll be fine . . . it takes a lot of core muscle strength, and it looks like you've got that. Do you lift and work out during the off-season?"

"I love running, so that's what I do. I just like that feeling of running six or eight miles. How calm and relaxed I am. I try to do pushups and sit-ups, things like that, but nothing that requires a gym. The gym is too boring, I guess."

Finn is done dressing and watches me intently as I gracelessly wrestle my jeans off from underneath the towel and pull the shorts on. Then I unwrap myself from the towel and tie the drawstring at my waist. I fold up all my clothes and the towel and set them on the trunk.

"You can leave them in the car if you want. I do it all the time. It's safe," Finn says, getting the boards down from the roof of the car. I place everything neatly on top of the scattered collection of bags, shoes, sandals, and clothes on the backseat. Finn locks the car, then he grabs one of the boards and tucks it under his arm like all the surfers do in movies. I do the same.

"And we're off," he declares. He starts down one of the paths, his feet kicking the dry, white sand as he walks. Finally, we come over the last dune and the beach appears before us. It is empty.

"It's usually not this empty, but the sun is really hot today, and there's little breeze," Finn says. "We'll have it to ourselves for a couple of hours."

Finn is a patient teacher. He explains that the first thing is always to sit and watch: watch what the other people are doing, where they are sitting, and how far out they paddled.

"Yeah," I say. "So many people for me to learn from." I laugh.

"Okay," he laughs and bumps me with his elbow. He stands beside me, each of us holding our boards upright in the sand, and he points with an outstretched arm toward the water, explaining what he sees. "Then watch where and how the waves break. See that top? That's the break. It curls into a lip, then when it finally closes, it's the tube. On really tall waves, like out in California, they have a pocket. There are pockets here too, just not big enough for us to stand in. So you'll want to ride the face of the wave, that kind of vertical spot right beneath the peak over here." His arm slowly slides to the right. "First though, you can't ride a wave until you've learned how to stand."

Before even getting in the water, he has me practice lying on the ground and then getting up and standing. He draws an outline of a surfboard in the sand and I practice standing in the middle of it. I feel foolish, and he laughs when I say so. "Yeah, you look kind of stupid, but trust me, you'll be glad you did this at least a couple of times when we get out there."

Feeling ready to get in the water, we wrap on our ankle straps, pick up our boards, and head out. We march into the surf with our boards held vertically in front of us, the cold waves splashing against our legs, forcing us back.

"The tide is coming in," Finn yells over his shoulder to me. "Wait until you are waist deep, and then get on top of it."

Then he takes two large steps, drops his board on the water, and jumps on top of it. I follow his lead but can't keep up with him as he paddles out about a hundred feet. When he stops, he sits up and turns his head to check that I've made it. It's surprisingly hard work, but I finally make it out to him. As I am sitting up, the water swells beneath us, and I lose my balance. I'm in the water before I can react. It takes me three attempts to get back up on my board. I rest my head on my board, panting. I haven't even tried to catch a wave yet.

"Arch your head up so the water passes between you and the board," Finn suggests. "You ready? 'Cause now comes the hard part."

I arch up my head and say, "I'm ready."

"But are you having fun?"

Since Dad died, everyone always asks if I'm okay but never if I'm having fun. In all the time we have hung out, Finn has never asked if I was fine, if I wanted to do something else. He just assumed I was okay or I wouldn't be there. For the first time since I had come to the beach this summer, I felt less lost, less without focus.

"Yeah," I said. "I'm having fun."

"Great. Just try and ride your first waves on your stomach or sitting up. Save standing for later. When you do feel ready to stand, just go for it. Pop up to your feet, forget going to your knees first." After giving me that last piece of advice, he goes off, leaving me to work out what he has just said.

I paddle back and forth, trying to catch the waves but miss them. My arms start to burn, and I swallow more seawater than I have in my entire life. I try going from my stomach, to sitting upright, to back on my stomach again to catch a wave. Once, I almost catch a wave, and I ride it for about fifty feet, but eventually the entire ocean runs beneath me, as if I'm anchored to the earth at this one place.

Finally, I'm done, exhausted. My arms are sore, and despite how hard I try, how deep I dig into the water, I cannot get the board to move anymore. I sit upright, feeling my heartbeat beneath my chest. I have not worked this hard in months.

I watch as Finn, fifty feet to my left and another fifty further from the shore, sits with his board facing toward me, but his head is turned back, scanning the open ocean for a wave to catch. His chest fills in and out with each breath, and his shoulders ripple as he shifts his weight from side to side. Without warning, he falls flat to his stomach and the board moves as if on a motor while his arms slice through the water with even, alternating strokes. The wave comes up from behind him, and as the board starts to tilt forward and the wave swells and grows, he stands. He keeps his feet apart and his shoulders and body upright. His legs and the board move as if they are one, swiveling beneath his hips.

The wave is now closer to me, and I feel myself start to tilt toward shore. Lost in watching him catch the wave, I forget it will also eventually reach me. Before Finn is even parallel to me, my board starts to upend itself, and I fall into the white water surrounding me. The leash on my ankle pulls me again, and the water tumbles me. I swim toward what I think is the surface, expecting to feel my arms break through to the air, but the surface never comes. The leash keeps pulling on my foot, the water swirls around me, and then my shoulder hits sand. I tumble, the water pulling me across the gritty bottom. I start to wonder if my lungs won't burst. I don't know how, but suddenly I feel the ocean floor beneath my feet. Standing upright, my head breaks the surface, just barely, before the leash on my ankle yanks my foot again, and my head is back under water as I tumble aimlessly. I stand again, this time in water that barely rises to my waist as the wave continues past me. I stumble forward, the board yanking on my ankle, and I realize my shorts have come off my waist and are wrapped around my knees. I fall forward, hitting my face against my board, and once more the waves drag me against the bottom, this time on my chest. The water rushes past me, back toward the ocean, and I get to my hands and knees to try to stand. My suit has my knees bound together, so I fall to my stomach and roll onto my back.

After about a minute I hear Finn's feet slap the wet sand as he runs toward me. I sit up. My chest is covered in seaweed, sand sits thick and splotchy on my stomach, buried in the hair on my stomach and legs. I hear Finn rip the Velcro from his ankle strap and feel his hands on my shoulders as he kneels beside me.

"Here, let's get you up and closer to shore," Finn says, and puts his arms underneath my shoulders to drag me into the white sand. Then he hauls me up and I turn to face him.

"You in there?" he asks, and smiles. He kneels down and tries to untwist my shorts, but they are wrapped so tightly around my legs I nearly fall over again. I place my hand on his back to help keep my balance and slowly step my legs out of my shorts. I straighten them out and get them back up over my hips. The tie string is gone, and there is a huge rip exposing my right thigh, and I imagine, half my butt. I stand on my own, but I'm wobbly and almost fall forward.

Finn stands, grabbing me tightly by my shoulders to steady me. His eyes are huge and his smile is gone. "Are you hurt?"

I smile and shake my head. With my right hand, I pull my shorts up against my waist, and with my other hand, I wipe some sand from my face. Finn hesitantly smiles back. "Well, you don't look too good."

"I know," I reply, "But I'm fine."

It takes ten minutes of arguing before I convince Finn to go back out and surf some more. He keeps asking if I want to head to the car or if I am hurt anywhere. He explains how he had decided to catch that wave, never thinking about me. He repeatedly apologizes, taking blame for my inexperience, saying he should have never left me alone.

But I just keep stating the same thing over and over again: I am okay, and I knew that, this being my first time ever surfing, I was going to wipe out. Finally, because I'm getting tired and annoyed, I say, "I have survived worse crashes." And that ends it all.

Finn catches three more waves, which takes about another forty minutes. I sit on the beach and watch, eventually getting up and walking back into the water to rinse off all the sand. My shorts have no intention of staying on my waist, so I continually pull them up. I watch Finn surf. Occasionally, he looks at me on the shore, checking to make sure I am okay. I wave, and he smiles, waves back, and turns his head back toward the ocean. When he catches a wave, I marvel at how easy he makes it look, especially after the pounding I just took. When Dad would watch me run at cross-country meets, he would tell me how fluid I looked, how relaxed I appeared. I wish he were here so I could tell him that I finally understood what he was seeing in me; what it was like to watch someone do what he loves and be in awe of his ability. I smile a bit, because this is the first time it has felt okay for me to miss Dad.

Finally, Finn rides a wave all the way to the shore. He slows down as the water moves back out toward the ocean, and with one smooth and graceful move, he hops off the board as it slides below the water. He bends over, pulls his board up and heads toward me. As he approaches, I can tell he has a sunburn. Neither of us had bothered to put on any sunscreen. I will be burnt tonight and maybe tomorrow, but I know in a day or two it will blend in with the tan I already have.

"Your face is bright red," I say, as he drives his board into the ground and spins around to sit beside me, facing the water.

"You should see yourself. Not only are you burnt, but you have giant raspberries on your chest and shoulders."

"Yeah, I could feel them. Not going to be fun tomorrow."

"When I first started, I was just one giant scab, you know. I wiped out like that every day. For some reason, I stuck with it." I ask if he surfed alone or with friends. He says there are a bunch of guys who surf down a bit closer to the pier, but usually he went out by himself. A couple of summers ago, he met a girl from California who spent the summer here with her cousins. She surfed with him a bit. "She was excellent, better than any of the guys here. This was so simple for her. I learned a lot from her that summer."

I say we should probably get out of the sun. With one hand holding up my shorts, I grab my board with the other hand. Finn offers to carry the board for me, but I refuse because I feel guilty for destroying his swimming suit. We get back to the car, and Finn starts to put the boards back on the roof. I try to help put the boards away, but every time I take my hand from the waist of my shorts, they drop to the ground. It is a bit of a joke, and we keep laughing about it. I tell him I will buy him another pair of shorts, but he keeps declining. "You know how many pairs of board shorts I own?"

Once the boards are secured, Finn opens the car door. I tell him he can have the towel to change since he is wet and needs to dry off. I step behind the door like he did hours before and hand him the towel from the backseat. Deciding not to be so self-conscious this time, I simply let go of my shorts and they fall to my ankles. I have dried sand on my stomach, in my hair, along my arms and legs, so I brush it off as best I can. Then I duck down to reach into the backseat to pick up my neatly folded clothes.

"Your scars stand out more when you're burnt," Finn says quietly.

I glance back at him to see him with the towel wrapped around his waist, staring at me. Holding my pants in my hand, I rotate my arm and hand to look at my scars.

"Actually, I meant the one on your head," Finn says, and drags his hand along the top of his own head.

I kind of laugh and want to say I know exactly where the scar is. The doctor said my stitches would burn and itch, and it was all I could do not to scratch them after I got home from the hospital. After about three weeks, I finally had a light covering of hair, but the scabs and stitches kept getting caught in it. When it was finally time to get the stitches taken out, I sat in the doctor's chair for almost forty minutes as he snipped away both the thread and the hair from my head.

"It's like, bright, bright pink," Finn continues. "Did you go through the windshield or something?"

I run my fingers through my hair and follow the scar to where it just barely appears on my forehead. "No. I was in my seatbelt. And all the windows shattered when the car started rolling. I don't know how it happened. I think I hit my head against the edge of the window or something."

Finn says, "You must feel lucky that you only cut your head and not your face, or that all the glass didn't get in your eye or something."

This is the first time anyone has said that I had been lucky in the accident. Not knowing what else to say, I tell him I guess he's right. I continue to brush off the sand again, all the while trying to figure out if I really did feel lucky. I spent two weeks in the hospital and had to have surgery. I spent months on crutches and with stitches and bandages on my head. I now have pins in my hand and wrist.

Oh, and let's not forget Dad died. One moment we were in the car together, and then he was gone. What was so lucky about any of that?

Suddenly, the towel hits me in the face. I pull it off to see Finn pulling his jeans up over his bare thighs. "Here, use this to brush the sand off you. Trust me, you do not want a fine layer of sand caught between you and your clothes slowly scraping the skin off your body."

I stand there, almost angry that he has the nerve to bring up the accident, my scars, and Dad's death, and then quickly move on to being normal because it doesn't affect him. His throat doesn't close and go dry at the thought of Dad being dead. His stomach doesn't tighten during dinner each night as Aunt Marion tries to make trite, pointless conversation instead of just letting the oppressive silence overwhelm us. Since coming to the beach this summer, I have spent hours sitting in the sun on the beach, then come home to shower and sit on the porch with everyone, my wet hair plastered against my head. Mom, Aunt Marion, Liam, none of them has ever mentioned the bright pink scar, or the ones on my wrists and foot. Or the accident. We just ignore it all, wishing it all into non-existence.

Part of me is angry that Finn made me think of my scars. Next, he might ask about my surgeries, and after that, the weeks I spent on crutches where I hobbled through school, ignoring the stares in the cafeteria. Or how the teachers who never even seemed to know my name were suddenly super kind and asked me if I needed any extra help with homework.

Then he will want to talk about the accident. Was it the wet roads or the other car that caused it? Whose side of the car was hit first? And how many times did we roll? And finally, why in the hell did Dad die when it was my side of the car that crashed into the concrete pylons? All the thoughts I've had but never shared with anyone, all of them could suddenly come out. Part of me doesn't think I'm ready for that.

But part of me is so relieved that someone is willing to say, "It happened."

Chapter 8

On Saturday morning, Aunt Marion gets Liam and me out of bed early—like eight a.m. She comes into our room with a pan and a wooden spoon, banging nosily as she calls our names. Liam throws his pillow at her but misses. She laughs and scurries out of the room. "You have guests coming tonight, so you need to help us clean the house and get ready," she calls as she heads down the stairs.

Liam gets out of bed and saunters to the bathroom without saying a word. He and I are still tormenting each over this dinner. Last night while we were eating, Liam asked, "Who is your friend again, Ty? The one coming for dinner tomorrow?" Mom and Aunt Marion stopped talking and looked at me. When I didn't say anything, Liam said, "Finn. That's his name, right?" The heat of a blush ran up my neck, so I only nodded and quickly stuffed a bite of quesadilla into my mouth.

"Well," Mom said before taking a long drink of her wine. "I guess with two special guests coming, we ought to do something special."

"I guess we will have to have a seafood dinner," Aunt Marion said.

I don't know what came over me, but what Aunt Marion said hit me harder than when Liam mentioned Finn's name. I started shaking all over and was too afraid to even pick up my glass of water, thinking I would spill it.

The seafood feast is my favorite tradition at the beach. We've done it every year since I can remember. It was something Dad started one rainy morning when everyone was sitting in the living room trying desperately to fill the overwhelming stillness that can be the beach. Dad was thumbing through a cooking magazine when he suddenly said, "How about steamed crabs tonight?" At the time, I thought he meant going out to eat, but then he walked over to the desk and hunted out a pencil and pad of paper. "At least, that's what I'm fixing. Tyler, what about you? What seafood do you want to make tonight?"

As I got older, the seafood feast evolved into a day-long event. We always picked a day in the middle of the week— Dad insisted we would get the best pick of fresh fish since the crowds were smaller compared to a weekend. As the day approached, we'd ask each other what they were going to pick, sometimes picking entrées that would go well together. On the day of the dinner, Mom and Aunt Marion would wash our good tablecloth and napkins and pull out our best dishes. Dad, Liam, and I always went to the market. Dad loved to chat with the fishmongers, asking when the catch came in, which fish were farmed, and which were wild caught. He never came with a list or recipe; he memorized what everyone wanted, and just knew what spices and sides to buy. What seasonings to throw in with the shrimp that evening as it sizzled in the cast-iron pan he always used. Which olive oil to baste the salmon with, and broccoli to go with the clams and pasta. He just knew in his head how the entire feast would come together. I was always in awe of how he could do that.

After Liam gets out of the shower, I quickly jump through one. The four of us eat breakfast together and decide what we are fixing for tonight. After Liam and I clean up the house and we all eat lunch, Liam, Aunt Marion, and I head down to the fish market. There are two levels. The first is open-air with vendors behind booths that are filled with pastas and vegetables, deep troughs of fish covered in chips of ice, or tables of spices in jars. Some vendors sell fresh-cut flowers or fresh-baked goods and desserts. One vendor passes out samples of chocolate pastas to visitors. Upstairs there are actual stores, more seafood and general grocery stores and some souvenir shops. Dad was right. It's a Saturday afternoon and the aisles are packed like I've never seen before. It's crowded, but low key.

Aunt Marion has a list of ingredients as we walk through the stalls. "I think," she says, spinning around, trying to figure out where we are, "the stand we always get crab legs from is over there." She points to a giant fish stand, one that is famous for the fishmongers throwing the orders over the heads of shoppers and making jokes with the customers. It is surrounded by tourists who are taking pictures on their phones. It is the exact opposite of where Dad would have shopped. I know Aunt Marion is trying. She never came with us before, and this is all new to her.

"It's not," I say. Then I take the list from her. My eyes well up just a bit as I try to make out the items we have to buy. "We bought crab legs at the store on the second floor. From Joe's Crab Shack. He always remembered us and knew Dad's name. Salmon, from the last stall at the end, down there." I point toward the far end of the aisle. Then I see mussels on the list.

"Mussels?" I ask. I actually don't think we have ever had mussels before. Not that I can remember. "We usually don't get mussels. So, I guess I don't know."

"Melissa wants them," Liam says. When I look up, he has his hands shoved in his pockets, and he just shrugs. Then he smiles, and I decide I can even tolerate Melissa for this. For the seafood feast. For Dad's Feast.

"Well," I say, leading the way toward the stairs. "First we hit Joe's. And I bet he can tell us the best place to get mussels." I am so excited about tonight that I literally sprint up the steps.

Two hours later we are back at the beach house. All the food we've bought clutters the kitchen, the fish in crates of ice on the floor, bags of pasta and vegetables filling the counters, and a bottle of wine for Mom and Aunt Marion in a pot of ice and cold water. Aunt Marion is setting up the dining room and has tasked Liam and I with the actual cooking. The ice that settled between us seems to be melting, because he and I laugh and tell stories from past seafood dinners as we peel shrimp and cut up vegetables. We take turns reading to each other the recipes we've looked up on our phones as we slowly figure out how to pull together everything we bought into a real meal.

Thirty minutes before Finn and Melissa are to arrive, Aunt Marion comes into the kitchen. "You two need to get changed," she says as she gently pushes us aside and peers into the pots and pans on the stove. Liam and I are in shorts and T-shirts, which I thought would be fine. Aunt Marion, however, is wearing a nice pair of dress slacks and a cream-colored blouse.

"Hurry now. You don't want to make your guests wait." She shoos Liam and I out of the kitchen. "I've got it from here." As we are heading up the stairs, Mom starts to come down. She is wearing a light summer dress, tastefully patterned with seashells and fish. Her hair is combed and flowing down her shoulders. We have to stop to let her pass, and as she does, she runs her fingers through both our hair. Liam puts his hand on my shoulder, and says, "I'm sorry, Ty, but I'm wearing your shirt and tie." Then he runs up the steps.

"Dude," I call out after him. "Then what am I going to wear?" I sprint up after him.

When Finn and Melissa arrive, Melissa is holding a pie.

"We brought dessert," Finn announces.

"Well," Melissa laughs, "actually, Finn brought it, and he told me as we were walking up the stairs that we could say we both brought it."

"If you hadn't said anything, we would never have known," Liam says lightly.

"Well, it's a kind gesture, both of you," Aunt Marion says, taking the pie and heading to the kitchen.

Halfway through dinner, Aunt Marion is telling a story about a time when we had a giant tuna for the seafood dinner. She pulls a photo album from the bookshelf and flips through to a photo from that year. It's of Liam and I trying to carry the tuna from the car into the house. The tuna is bigger than we are, and the two of us are hugging it to our chests, trying to keep it from touching the ground. We might be around ten. Liam and I cringe as the book gets passed around, but it's all in good fun. When dinner is finally over, Aunt Marion starts to collect the plates.

"Here," Finn says, "let me help with those. I need to get the dessert ready in the kitchen, so I'm heading that way anyway."

As Finn heads into the kitchen with a stack of dinner plates, Aunt Marion turns to Mom and mouths, "What a gentleman." On her way to the kitchen, she playfully slaps the top of Liam's head and whispers, "You could take some pointers, young man."

Finn brings out the pie, which turns out to be key lime. "A good one," he says. "Not like what you get in those expensive tourist bakeries downtown. This one's homemade by my neighbor, what we townies have." We eat and laugh. Finn tells stories about what it's like to live in Stone Harbor year-round, and he and Aunt Marion reminisce about old buildings that are gone and the time when the boardwalk flooded and the city decided to not rebuild it.

"Honestly," Finn says, "I actually don't remember that. But my parents talk about it."

"I think he just called us old, Maureen," Aunt Marion laughs.

Mom just smiles and compliments Finn on the pie again. "It was really delicious. You should thank your neighbor for us."

"When I heard that this dinner was a tradition, I decided to bring one of my own. Or at least, a Stone Harbor one. How did you start this, anyway?"

For a moment, no one says anything. I am about to tell the story of our first feast on that rainy day when Dad decided we would each pick a meal, but Aunt Marion chimes in and shrugs, and says, "Oh, I don't remember. It just seems like something we've always done."

Then Mom excuses herself, saying she has a headache. The rest of us finish our pie in silence.

Liam and Melissa stroll down the boardwalk holding hands. Finn and I walk about three feet behind them. Not long after Mom left for her room, Aunt Marion very abruptly brought the dinner to an end. "If I don't start cleaning up the kitchen now," she said, "I'll be at it all night. Why don't you kids go out and have some fun?"

Like always, we go to Wildwood. Melissa is giggling and laughing so hard she sometimes pulls Liam off balance, which only makes both of them laugh harder. As they pass one of the boardwalk games, Melissa stops short and points toward a toy sea lion hanging against the wall. She pulls Liam toward the booth, and he digs into his pocket to get his wallet.

"I guess Liam's about to show off his manly skills," Finn says, and takes a step toward the two.

I don't follow him, because I'm seething over what just happened.

The seafood dinner was going perfectly, in my opinion. We were having fun, we were telling stories. The day spent getting ready was the best day we've had this summer. It was just like having Dad here, even though he isn't. And when no one wanted to mention him when Finn asked how we started the tradition, it was ruined. It's obvious that Liam, Aunt Marion, and Mom think the best thing we can do is never mention him again.

But I can't do that.

I reach out and grab Finn's arm and say, "It was Dad's idea."

He stops and gives me a lost look. "Okay," he nods. "What was?"

"The seafood dinner. No one said so when you asked, and I don't know why because it is the single best thing about coming to the beach. Every year, Dad would set a date, and we would each get to pick one dish. Whatever it was we wanted. And then he would come up with an entire recipe for each dish. Then we'd go down to the market and buy all the ingredients. It was always a good time, just like tonight. And it was his idea. All of it."

"It's a good idea. I like that you still do it. I'm glad you told me. So, which course did you pick? I bet it was the shrimp, right?"

I hear his question, but I can't answer it. Because I finally start to see how alone I am in all of this. I watch Liam as he throws a softball at milk jugs to win a stuffed animal. I mean, he is completely unfazed by what just happened tonight. Obviously, Finn's question hit Mom hard too, but her reaction was to disappear. That's basically been her response all summer. I thought Aunt Marion might say something, but she didn't. In fact, she kind of lied. Because we all knew the answer.

I start to shake uncontrollably, and a knot quickly forms in my throat. I'm about to lose it completely in the middle of the boardwalk. I need a place to go, but where? I spin around and there are steps leading to the beach, and I nearly sprint down them. Finn follows. I make it to the edge of the water, where the lights from the rides and the booths don't reach, and stop.

Then I just let go. I cry. Not just a couple of tears, but an exhausting cry, pushing all the air from my lungs. At first, Finn just stands there, but when I don't stop, he turns me to face him and puts his hands on my shoulders. I keep crying, not saying anything, and not really thinking anything except I hate that I'm crying and I want to stop. But the more I try, the more I realize I can't. Then Finn hugs me, pulling me against his chest, patting my back with one hand and holding my head tight against him with the other.

"Hey," he whispers. "Hey. It's okay." He pushes back from me and gently tilts my face up to be level with his. "What just happened back there?"

"I can't be like them. I need to remember him. Because if I don't . . . " I run out of breath and after a quick gulp say, ". . . I don't know. That's just the thing. I don't know how to be without him. How to enjoy running again. How to smell coffee and not think of him. How not to look forward each year to that stupid seafood dinner. And at the same time never wanting to go through it again, not like that. I don't know how to be me without him here anymore."

Then, out of nowhere, I hear Liam calling my name. "Tyler!

Where'd you go? Hey, you guys out there?" I can tell he's walking along the beach looking for us. His voice gets closer each time he calls out.

"They can't see us in the dark this far out," Finn says as he starts to spin around. But I pull him back.

"No," I whisper. "I just can't be with them right now."

"Okay," Finn says. He wipes my face with the sleeve of his shirt and grabs me by my hand. "Come on, this way." He leads me along the surf, back north along the beach toward where we parked. When he is sure we are out of sight of Liam and Melissa, we head back onto the boardwalk. Once we enter the lights, Finn drops my hand, and we walk side by side. We eventually reach the car, and without thinking, I hand him the keys and walk over to the passenger side. We haven't said a single word the entire time, but I'm fine with that. Finn drives us back across Egg Harbor, and as he pulls onto Second Avenue, I realize he's taking me home.

"No," I plead. "Let's go somewhere else."

"Okay," Finn says, the word long and drawn out, trying to decide where else to go. He continues up Second Avenue until we reach the end of the island. He drives into a public parking lot and pulls into a spot close to the water and turns off the car.

"I'm sorry," I choke out and wipe my eyes.

"It's okay," He grabs my hand and gives it a hard squeeze.

"I just wanted that dinner to be . . . different."

"Who wouldn't?" he asks. "But I'm glad we did it, because I had fun."

I start to cry again, but this time not as hard. I close my eyes and rest my head against the window. Finn keeps holding my hand.

I wake up when Finn starts the car.

"Hey," I say, rubbing the sleep from my eyes. "I fell asleep."

"That's okay. I kind of did too." He pulls out of the parking lot and starts down Second Avenue toward the beach house.

I look down at the clock; it is five after one. Then I remember that Liam and Melissa are still on the boardwalk without a car.

"Shit," I say as I pull out my phone and scroll through my new texts, all from Liam. There are ten, and start with "Dude, where are you?" They go from being concerned and if I'm okay to the last at twelve thirty a.m. saying, "Hey, leaving us without a ride is bullshit." Then I have one missed call, but no message.

"What?" Finn asks.

"Liam and Melissa. We left them in Wildwood without a car."

"So . . . " Finn says. "What do we do? Where do you think they are?"

"Hopefully, Liam got them back to Stone Harbor, dropped off Melissa, and then got himself home," I say. "If not, I'll have to go get them. But first, we have to drive you home." I call Liam, but it goes straight to voicemail. I pause for a second, thinking of what to say. I can't think of anything, so I hang up.

"You don't need to drive me. I walked to dinner tonight, remember?" Finn says. "If I were Liam, I'd be pissed. Like, really pissed. Can you see if he made it home?"

I shake my head. "I don't know, he isn't answering his phone . . . "

"'Cause if he isn't," Finn continues, "you need to go find him soon. And driving me home first doesn't make that happen any faster." By this time, we're at the beach house, and Finn pulls the car into the driveway.

"I'll be fine, really," he says. I must still look uncertain because he grabs my phone from my hand and texts himself. "Tell you what. Here's my number. If something scary happens, I'll call you." He smiles, but when I don't smile back, he changes his tone. "Seriously, go in and see if he's there. If not, call me. Then come pick me up and we can go look for him together. Otherwise, I'm betting he's inside, sound asleep." Then he hands me back my phone, tousles my hair, and gets out of the car.

I get out, walk around to the other side of the car, and give him a hug. Then I whisper "thanks" into his ear. He heads toward the sidewalk, and I go into the beach house through the kitchen door. Aunt Marion is putting a glass into the dishwasher. I look at my phone, and I'm thirty minutes past curfew.

"Hey," I say, not sure what else to say.

"There you are," she says slowly. "Liam said you were going to be a little later than him."

"Yeah," I say, then pause. "I had to drive Finn home."

"Of course," she responds, but I know she doesn't believe either of us. "You look awful, Tyler. Go to bed."

When I get to the third floor, I see the door to the other bedroom is closed, and that Liam's bed in our room is empty, again. I get out of my clothes, crawl into bed, and fall asleep.

Chapter 9

It's been four days since what I now call the Seafood Fiasco, and Liam hasn't said a word to me about ditching him and Melissa on the boardwalk that night. In fact, we pretty much have stopped spending time together and speaking to one another. Now that I have Finn's number, he and I make plans on our own. I'm positive that Liam is hanging out with Melissa, which is fine by me.

I've slept in late today, so it's just after one p.m. by the time I get out of the shower. I'm standing in the bedroom with a towel wrapped around my waist trying to decide what to wear. As I pull on a blue shirt with a collar, the door to the spare bedroom swings open and Liam groggily shuffles to the bathroom in a pair of boxers. We don't even acknowledge each other. I quickly finish dressing and head downstairs so I'm gone by the time he finishes showering.

Besides, I have to grab a quick lunch because I'm going to meet Finn in a few minutes. I woke up forty minutes ago because he texted me to say he got off work at one p.m. today, but after that he was going up to Atlantic City to check out a new surf shop that opened. Did I want to go with him? He said we could also grab dinner up there, hang out a little bit, and then come back to Stone Harbor for a party tonight that some of his friends are having. I wrote back that I'd go and he can pick me up after he's done at work.

To be honest, I think having Finn around is exactly what I

wanted from this summer. I still have those moments where I'm suddenly overwhelmed by a memory of Dad, but they're somehow easier with him. Like yesterday, Finn and I headed to a wildlife preserve up near Atlantic City. He said it had a bird sanctuary, and since I mentioned walking around Bunker Pond that first time we went to the Cape May Lighthouse, he thought I might like it.

It was pretty great, actually. We hiked along this woodland trail to the base of an observation tower. We climbed up and sat on a bench to watch the sun go down. That's when it hit me. This is the exact type of thing Dad would have made us all do; he loved things like this. But we never came here. I don't think he even knew about it. I just couldn't get it out of my head that Dad would never see this place.

Finn reached out and started to rub my back. He must have known what I was thinking. I was preparing for him to ask if I was okay, or just say we should leave. Instead he asked, "So, what are you thinking?"

I decided to just tell him. "Dad would have loved this."

"I bet. It's kind of beautiful." He put his arm around my shoulder, and we finished watching the sunset.

We decided to go to Pizza Open for dinner. We hung out with some of his friends and played some video games. I made it home at 1:15 a.m. Liam's door was open when I climbed into bed, but not five minutes later I heard him coming up the steps and head into his room.

Now, I make a sandwich and head out to the porch. Aunt Marion is there, setting up her easel.

"Your mom's going to take a nap, but then I thought we could all go out tonight for dinner."

"Can't," I say between bites. "I'm going to a surf shop with

Finn in Atlantic City. We'll hang out there, grab some dinner, and just do whatever." I purposely avoid mentioning the party.

"What about Liam?"

"I'm pretty sure he has plans with Melissa."

"Guess that makes your mom and me the old maids." Aunt Marion laughs. "It's okay. You boys should be out having fun, not sitting around with your aunts. Just be safe. And," she adds warningly, "be back at a decent time tonight. I'll tell Liam the same thing."

The party is in Avalon, a small, ritzy neighborhood just north of Stone Harbor. Finn parks his car on the street at the end of the driveway, and then we walk up to the front door. The house is right along the beach, just like the one from the party where I met Finn, but bigger. Finn holds open the door for me, and as I go in I decide it's basically a repeat of that same party. Loud music, kids running around and goofing about. I think I even recognize some of the people. Finn walks around and introduces me to some kids he knows. We wander into the living room and Finn motions toward a guy standing alone against the wall with a drink in his hand.

"I used to surf with him," Finn says, "but not so much anymore. Let's go say hi."

We make our way through the crowd and Finn introduces me. They spend a few minutes just catching up, but they quickly start to talk about surfing. Finn ends up telling the story of taking me surfing for the first time. He tells it well, to be honest, but when he recounts my "epic wipeout," as he now calls it, they both laugh.

The other surfer notices I don't laugh. "I'm sorry," he

chuckles, patting me on the shoulder. "It's just that it happens to everyone on their first wave. You should have seen my first wipeout."

"Actually, it wasn't Tyler's first wave," Finn interjects. "He caught a couple of waves before that happened." He seems to be bragging and he shoots me a sideways grin. "So, you did better than most on your first try."

He's lying. I never caught a thing, but I just shrug.

"Right on," the surfer dude says, and bumps fists with me. "Come on, let's go get some drinks."

We enter the kitchen, Finn ahead of me, and the surfer behind me. My heart drops to my stomach when I see Melissa and Liam talking to a group of people next to the fridge. They look over as the three of us enter the room, and all the conversation stops for a second.

Melissa marches up to us and pushes Finn aside so she can point a finger in my face. "You shouldn't have left us like you did that night. We searched all over for you. We had to call a cab to get home!"

I laugh, even though I know I shouldn't. I mean, it's the first time the four of us have seen each other since then so there is no way to avoid some awkwardness, but for her to just attack me like this in public is kind of childish, in my opinion. "Really? A cab. Your biggest worry was riding home in a cab? Because what, you're such a spoiled brat you've never had to ride in one before? And all those other nights you two ditched us, did you ever wonder how we got home?"

She just crosses her arms over her chest and glares at me.

I turn to Liam. "The truth is, I never meant to leave you there. I fell asleep, and once I woke up, I tried to get ahold of you. I tried calling and texting and was even about to drive back to Wildwood to try and find you."

"Asleep. Yeah, right," Liam laughs.

"It's true," Finn says. "As soon as we woke up, he was in a panic trying to get ahold of you."

"Oh, of course you were there." Liam leans against the counter and rolls his eyes. "I mean, Jesus, if you two wanted to be alone so badly, you should have just said so instead of just ditching us. It's not like I'm going to care or tell anyone about it. I mean, I'm trying like hell to make it . . . normal. But whatever."

My mind is blown by what he just said. What is he trying to make seem normal? Is it normal to ditch your cousin all summer? Especially after his dad dies? And how normal is it that Liam barely mentions the accident or what it has done to us? As far as I know, the only time he has talked about the accident, it was with Melissa. The first time he met her. Anger boils in my veins as I picture him being all gallant and sensitive as he talks about me—his poor, orphaned cousin who needs to adjust to life without his dad—in an attempt to win her over. He used me to get to her.

"What's normal about anything any of us have done this summer?" I yell. "There's no way to make it normal because it's not. We pretend nothing has happened and no one will talk about it. If you want to try to be normal, try talking to me about it instead of her!"

"Of course he talks to me about it," Melissa yells back. "I'm who he is supposed to talk about it with!"

She's gone too far now. I've known Liam since I can remember, and she thinks one summer of cooing and kissing gives her the right to talk to him about Dad's death and how it's tearing the two of us apart? She is too out of line. I've held back all summer whenever she's pissed me off, but I'm done with that.

"You should just be quiet!" I shout. "This has nothing to do with you, Melissa. And it never will. So just shut it!"

"Maybe," Finn says, stepping between Melissa and me, "we should leave." He puts his hand on my shoulder to try and calm me down.

"Not maybe," I say. "Definitely."

"Liam is worried about you," Melissa shouts before we can leave. "And he doesn't know what to do about it. That's why he talks to me! And because . . . I mean . . . you could say it's my fault that it happened. It makes me feel guilty that if I hadn't met Liam, maybe none of this would be happening." She pauses. "And Finn's as much to blame for it as I am."

I'm so lost—I have no idea what Melissa is talking about. What is her fault? The accident? How does that even make sense? And why drag Finn into this? She is so self-centered it pisses me off

The look on Finn's face tells me he feels the same. Then he spins back to Melissa.

"And what do you mean by that? You'd better be really careful with what you say next." Finn's shoulders are tense. I've never heard him sound so angry.

Melissa's lips quiver, and as the tears build up in her eyes, she steps behind Liam.

"Jesus," Liam sighs. "Look, it isn't you. Seriously, I don't care who you are, or who you like. Truly, it's not like that. But really, did you ever think about him?" Liam points at me. "Did you ever think about what he's going through? I mean, it isn't like he's in the best of places. It's so hard for me to just sit back and do nothing. So hard. Do you know how much I love him? He's my only cousin, for God's sake. So, I need to ask you now: did you ever think about him before you . . . " His voice breaks, and he swallows hard. We all wait for him to say more, but he never finishes.

"Before what?" Finn whispers between his teeth.

"Before," Liam falters. "Before you swooped in and tried so hard to make him your boyfriend!"

It's as if space opened up and sucked all the air and sound from the room. It is eerily silent, and I struggle to catch my breath. It feels like someone has kicked me squarely in the chest. I stagger backward. Finn stares at me, and his mouth is open but not saying a word. I just look at him, confused. For a few seconds, nothing happens.

Finn finally breaks his gaze with me and spins around toward Liam. He takes two big steps into the kitchen. As he nears Liam, he cocks his arm back and makes a fist. Liam puts his arms up to cover his face. With Melissa standing behind him he can't move backwards, so he leans forward trying to duck the blow that is coming.

Finn hits him squarely in the ear. Liam's head appears to launch from Finn's fist, his neck craning painfully to the side, then snapping back. He stumbles sideways, taking two or three steps to keep his balance. Liam looks dazed for a second, but eventually he straightens up. He's okay, but the way he is wincing we all know how much that punch hurt.

Melissa steps from behind Liam and charges at Finn, pummeling him on the chest with her fists. Finn just stands there. By now, a crowd has gathered, but all four of us are stuck in place—not moving, not saying anything. Finally, Melissa stops hitting Finn and says, "You'd better go."

Finn walks back across the kitchen and stops in front of me, as if to say something. He looks scared or even shocked. He opens his mouth, but then pushes past me and out the door.

Liam's ear is red and starting to swell. Melissa is getting ice from the freezer. The crowd is buzzing, and finally someone says to me, "Who was that kid? And why did he hit that other dude in the ear?"

"Fuck off," I say without even looking at him. I walk over to Liam, but he locks eyes with me and shakes his head. I turn and run through the rest of the house, slam through the front door and down the driveway. Finn is in his car, the engine running and the lights on, but not moving. I walk up beside it and knock on the passenger-side window. He looks over, and I try the door, but it's locked.

"Let me in," I say softly. He looks out the front windshield for a second, then he gives in and leans over to unlock the door. I climb in, and no sooner do I sit down, he pulls away, squealing his tires.

Finn drives back to town, never taking his eyes off the road. Finally, he pulls up to the end of Beach Drive where we park. He turns off the car and we just sit there. Not sure what to do, I look out my window at the houses.

"Tyler," Finn whispers.

He reaches out, puts his hand behind my head, and pulls me toward him. Our foreheads touch, our noses inches apart. I wait for him to say something. Suddenly he jerks away, puts his head against the headrest, and cries. I cannot think of anything to say, so I reach out and pull him toward me. He slides from behind the steering wheel, puts his head against my chest, and sobs into my shirt. I take a deep breath, close my eyes, and bury my face into his hair.

Chapter 10

I sit and hold Finn as he cries for what seems like an eternity. Trying desperately to think of what to say, I remember how he comforted me that night I lost it on the Boardwalk: he simply held me and kept saying I was okay. So I figure something similar. I stroke his hair and whisper onto the top of his head, "It's going to be all right."

"I really doubt that." He pries himself from my chest, wipes his eyes, and then looks me in the face. "You really have no clue." I open my mouth to respond, but he's right. I don't know what he's talking about, so I have nothing to say.

Finn spins around, curls up along the seat and props his head against my thigh. His eyes are closed, and he's breathing deeply. He's so still and stays like that for so long I thought he fell asleep. My thigh is falling asleep from the weight of his head, so eventually I whisper.

"Finn, are you asleep."

"No," he says flatly. Then he quickly adds, "What time is it?"

I fish my phone from my pocket and say, "1:35."

"Shit," Finn says as he sits up. "I guess I'll get you home."

By the time Finn drops me off, it's 1:50 a.m. As I walk up the front porch steps, digging through my pocket for my keys, I expect Aunt Marion to be up and waiting. I peek my head in through the door, and the front room is dark and empty.

I head toward the stairs and take a seat on the bottom one. I miss Dad. If he were alive, he'd be waiting for me. He'd be angry, but he'd also be concerned. Until this summer, I wasn't one to blow off curfew—that's more Liam's thing. Dad would want to know why I was late, and I try to have a conversation in my head with him: About what happened tonight. About what has been happening this whole summer. About Liam and Melissa. And Finn. Then I'd ask him what he thinks I should do.

It's no use, though. He's gone, and I don't know what to do.

I climb upstairs to my room. Liam's door is closed. I lie down and fall asleep.

Hours later, I wake up and see Liam's clothes from the day before sprawled on top of the dresser. Downstairs I can hear Aunt Marion talking. I get up to take a shower, but as I get to the bathroom, I can hear water running. Liam must be in there. I decide to use the outdoor shower, the one we use to rinse sand off before coming inside. I would rather go outside now than wait and have to see Liam when he exits the bathroom.

I realize that something Melissa said last night was actually right, in a way. I do blame her. But it's not for what she thinks. I blame her for splitting Liam and me apart. If the two of them think Finn stalked me, they were blind to how Melissa had done the same. Swooping in and clapping and cooing, she all but made sure she was his center of attention. Leaving me with Finn. He didn't chase me. As I see it, Liam was the one who pulled away from me. I was left alone. I had no one else but Finn.

Liam obviously plans to keep Melissa around, at least while he is here at Stone Harbor. I can make this all go away if I can convince Mom we should leave and head back to Chicago. I think through the reasons I can give her for heading home, but none of them are too convincing, even to me. Besides, I'm not sure I want to go back to Chicago.

Perhaps Liam and Aunt Marion can head back to Baltimore, but honestly there is no way Aunt Marion is leaving if Mom is staying here. I realize we are all stuck together.

I wrap my towel around my waist and grab my clothes. As I walk back into the kitchen, I find Mom, Aunt Marion, and Liam all at the table eating muffins and yogurt.

"There you are," Aunt Marion says. "Liam just told me you were still asleep in your room."

Liam stares at me with no particular expression on his face. He obviously went back to the room to change after his shower, and so he knows I wasn't asleep. My only guess is, he thought I had stayed out all night and was covering for me. I'm smart enough to play along. The less we say about what happened last night and what time we both got back, the better.

"No," I say. "I woke up just after he got into the shower and decided to take one outside instead of waiting."

"Well, sit," Aunt Marion commands, and she pulls a muffin from the serving tray and puts it on a small plate for me. "Juice?"

"Thanks," I say, and sit down at the table.

Aunt Marion gets up, and as she passes behind him, she notices Liam's swollen ear. "My god, Liam, is that stupid earring infected?"

Liam rolls his eyes. I'm sure he was hoping he could somehow get through the morning without her noticing it. I smirk because that was a foolish notion. I'm surprised it took Aunt Marion this long to notice how bruised and swollen it is.

"No, it's fine, Mom. I mean, the earring is nothing. You wouldn't believe it," he says. "I was standing in the kitchen at a friend's house last night, and some kid hit me in the ear."

"What?" Aunt Marion says. "Maureen, look at this." She turns Liam's head so Mom can look at his ear.

"That's pretty bad," Mom says. "Why did this boy hit you?"

"And who was it?" Aunt Marion asks, tilting Liam's head so she can get a better look at his ear.

"It was Tyler's . . . " Liam starts, looking right at me. My throat goes dry, and I can feel my heart racing in my chest. After what seems like an eternity, Liam continues, "It was Tyler's friend. I mean, it was an accident. He was just going about his business, and I was in the way. He was trying to get a glass out of the cupboard, and when he swung the door open, he hit me. I mean, honestly some of it is my fault. I was like, being where I shouldn't have been, know what I mean? But still, it hurt."

The entire time Liam is staring at me, making sure I get exactly what he is saying: He handled the whole situation badly, but Finn shouldn't have hit him.

"Well," Mom says, but nothing else.

Aunt Marion continues to examine Liam's head, then she touches his ear. "It looks horrible."

"Ouch!" Liam cries, and jerks his head from her hands. "Well, you mashing it around doesn't help it feel any better."

"Drop the drama. I think you need to go see a doctor."

"I'm fine, Mom." Liam rolls his eyes. "Weren't you getting Tyler some orange juice?"

"Okay, just a mother's right to be worried." Aunt Marion continues into the kitchen. "And it was Finn? That sweet boy who came to dinner the other night?" We hear her open the freezer and dig through the ice. She drops some ice in a glass, and finally I find my voice.

"He feels horrible about it," I say. Liam raises his eyebrows at me, then tears off a piece of his muffin and puts it in his mouth. "He told me last night, right after it happened. I mean, yeah, you were kind of being . . . it was mostly your fault, but still."

"Well," Liam says, and shrugs.

Aunt Marion comes back with a glass of orange juice for me

and a bag of ice for Liam. "Here." She hands the bag of ice to Liam. "Can you hear out of it?"

"Well, yeah," Liam says, "If I plug my other ear, I can still hear, but everything is kind of muffled." He puts the bag of ice to his ear and winces.

"Maureen, isn't there a doctor somewhere nearby on the mainland?" Aunt Marion asks as she sits back down.

"Dr. Kell," Mom answers. "His number is written in the desk somewhere." She gets up and walks into the living room, and we hear her going through the drawers of the bureau under the old landline phone we still have.

Aunt Marion says, "Liam, you should go see a doctor. It looks horrible, and what if the eardrum is ruptured, or something?" Liam nods, and we all sit in silence. After about ten minutes, Mom comes back into the room.

"I got him an appointment in forty-five minutes. You'll have to leave soon, though, because you can't be late. He's fitting you in between people."

"Okay," Liam says. "I should change, I'm in my swimming shorts." He gets up and starts to walk to the stairs. As he passes me, he stops. "What, are you a nudist now, going to just hang out in a towel all day?" He's trying to be subtle, but I get it. He wants me to go upstairs with him.

"I guess I am dry now," I say, and start to stand.

"But you haven't finished eating," Aunt Marion says, and points to my muffin and juice. I sit back down, and Liam leaves, knowing to wait for me to get up there. He doesn't need forty-five minutes to change into shorts and drive ten minutes to the mainland. And it would be more than acceptable if he did show up wearing his board shorts in a beach town.

When I get to the room, Liam is lying on his bed with his hands behind his head.

"So," he says. "You gonna say you're sorry?"

"Me? I'm not the one who hit you." I sit down on my bed, and almost add, Plus, you deserved it.

"Not for that," Liam says, sitting up. "That's between me and Finn. I was out of line, so I'll fix it." He takes a deep breath. "But you? Not a sorry . . . but something? You've been angry at me for . . . Actually, I don't know why, because you won't tell me. If I didn't know better, I would say you hate me for some reason."

"I don't hate you," I say.

"Who then? Melissa? Because she thinks you hate her. I know you do, but I'm sure as hell not going to tell her that."

"No, I don't hate her, either." I sigh. "But she obviously doesn't like me."

"She hardly knows you. How can she hate you?"

"Well, she definitely doesn't like having me around, that's obvious."

"No offense, Tyler, but you really haven't . . ." There is a long pause of silence. Finally, he looks away from me and says, "I hate to say this, Ty, but do you really think you are the only one who misses him? Because you aren't, you know that? I hate waking up every morning and not having his buckwheat pancakes. Man, I loved those."

Jesus, is he kidding me? "So sorry you cannot have pancakes. That must be awful," I drone.

"You see that?" He throws his hands in the air, exasperated. "Really, you think I was just talking about the pancakes? Or is it fun for you to be an ass? Because I miss him. I know you do too, but you aren't the only one."

This is insufferable, really. How the hell am I supposed to compare what I am going through with anything he's feeling? I mean, I know he meant something more than just pancakes, but still. Liam likes to complain about Uncle Ben—how hard he rides Liam, and the earring stunt is an example of how they live to push each other's buttons. But that's just the point, they're both still living. Liam gets to go home and see his dad. I don't. And ever since Dad died, the last thing I have tried to do is point that out to everyone.

Before I can even stop myself, I yell, "Do you realize there's not one thing about this place that doesn't just kill me because it reminds me of him? I can't do anything without thinking he should be here: eating dinner, going to the boardwalk, drinking coffee. I can't see a stupid magazine without thinking how he used to sit around all day reading them. I can't walk past the kite shop without remembering how much I hated that he always wanted to go in there, and I hate that I used to refuse to go in with him. It rips me apart. So yeah, you miss him, but I am dying. Literally."

"Good," Liam says, and leans forward with his elbows on his knees. "What else? Tell me, because I would love to know what you're thinking. I used to know, but I don't anymore."

I try to swallow the lump that has grown in my throat, and my eyes are watering. I understand what he wants me to do, but I can't. How do you tell someone you feel empty? That nothing has feeling anymore? I shrug.

"Okay," Liam says. "How about I tell you how I feel? Does that make it easier?"

"Yeah, sure," I whisper and wipe my nose.

"I miss your dad. I do. But as much as I miss him, I miss you too." He bites his lip and fights back tears. "I miss the Tyler who used to come here every summer and screw around with me. How we used to play videos in the arcade, or try to sneak beers from the fridge and run down to the beach to drink. Or sit on the roof and talk about high school and lacrosse and running and the girls we like. What I don't understand is why him being gone means you can't do that."

"Seems to me you have Melissa to do all that with. Well, except for the talk about girls part. It isn't like I haven't tried to talk to you."

"Liar," he says. "If I let you, you would just sit in silence and not say anything all day. I am busting my butt to find things for us to do—anything that you might like. And all I get is 'I don't care,' or, 'I don't know.' You don't even say no. And again, what do you have against Melissa? So I like her, big deal. And I want to be completely honest about how I feel about her . . . about liking someone, you know?" He slides further back on his bed. "I'm not sure you're being honest with me, or anyone else, to tell the truth."

"What is that supposed to mean?" But I know where he is going with this, and it makes my stomach ball up.

"You know exactly what I mean. At least I have the balls to tell you the truth about her. I've been dying to tell you more about how I feel about her. I mean, I know this is just a summer thing, but that's what makes it kind of fun, you know? But you don't even seem to care to talk to me. It seems the only person you talk to is Finn."

I don't say anything. Part of what he says is true. Right now, I really don't want to know about him and Melissa. First, she annoys me, and I think he could do better. I have never said that, but he must know that's how I feel. More importantly, though, ever since that first night we all met at the boardwalk, I feel like she and I are in a constant battle over Liam. She doesn't care that Liam and I are basically falling apart. I needed him this summer and she took him away from me.

But Finn? I'm not sure what to say.

"So, what about Finn?" Liam whispers, bringing me from

my thoughts. From the look on his face, I can tell he's not sure if he should have asked or not. I laugh, because that is one thing I have always admired about Liam—even when he isn't sure if it is the right thing to do, he just commits to it and does it. And most of the time it turns out to be the right thing.

"There's nothing about . . . " I start to say, but that's all I can get out before I start to cry. I drop my head into my hands, and let out a long sob. Liam comes and sits beside me and pulls my head onto his shoulder.

"I hate . . . being here . . . " I say between breaths. "And I hate everyone asking me if I am okay, and if everything is all right. Because the answer is no, nothing is all right. Why doesn't everyone just figure that out? But there is nothing you can do about it, so stop asking."

"Okay," Liam says. "Fine. But what does that have to do with Finn?"

"He's the only one who hasn't asked any of those questions. He just says, 'I'm going . . . wherever. Surfing or to a party or anywhere, so come along if you want.' And if I say no, he doesn't suddenly change his mind. He goes without me. I know that I can answer him and he won't try to read into it. He treats me like a normal person, not like the guy whose dad just died."

I sit up and use the towel around my waist to wipe my face.

"And I don't do that?"

"No. I know you want to, or you try to. But you don't."

"And that's it? So that's why you like having him around?" Liam asks. Then adds quickly, "I mean, just for that?"

I sigh and wipe my face again. It takes a second before I can find the words. "Yes, for all those reasons, I just like having him around. All I wanted out of this summer was for everything to be like it was before. But it isn't. It never will be like it was before. I get that now. It sucks, but turns out it's okay. And although I'm not sure exactly why it's okay, I know Finn has something to do with it. Everything is okay with Finn because . . . He's just . . . "

I have to stop, because what I am about to say next feels like a huge release. "It's because you're right: There is something more than just that." I take a deep breath, close my eyes and finally say, "I like Finn. I like how me makes me feel."

Neither of us says anything for a bit. Liam just puts his arm around my shoulder and pulls me tight against him.

"That's cool," he finally says. "Really. Despite how I sounded last night, I really like him. And you can tell, he really likes you. And if you're both happy, then Jesus, I'm happy for you."

"Yeah, well, last night certainly seemed different."

"I know. And this is no excuse, but it was because I was scared." Liam sighs. "I was scared because this summer was going to be hard for you, no matter what. I watched this all happening between you and Finn, and I knew what it was. Or I think I did. And I kept waiting for you to say something. If this had been any other summer, I think you would have already told me all this. And I'd be there for you. But that didn't happen."

I hear him sniff, and then he pulls his arm from around my shoulder and wipes his face.

"Ever since your dad died, all I've wanted to do is just . . . protect you, you know? Like, pull you in so close that nothing would ever hurt you again. That's what I pictured when Mom told me we were coming for the entire summer. I kind of had this idea that you and I were just going to spend all our time together, and that was the best thing I could do for you. But by the time I got here, you were so distant already. And then came Melissa. And then Finn. And I got scared."

He fiddles with the seam of his shirt. "I mean, maybe in

Chicago things are different, but back at my school in Baltimore? Two guys on my lacrosse team are dating. No one on the team cares, because it's not a big deal. Some kids in school, they tease them a lot. Sometimes they're actually mean. The guys on the team do what we can to be supportive. But it's still hard on them. It still hurts. I kept picturing that happening to you, and there was not a damn thing I could do about it."

He drops backward onto his elbows, stretching out across my bed. "You're the closest thing I have to a brother, Tyler, and I just figured we told each other everything. I mean, I do. I tell you just about everything, and I figured you did the same. And I feel a bit guilty, and a little angry, because I know you haven't been telling me anything."

I don't say a word. Because as much as I love Liam—and I do think of him as my brother—he's wrong. I am not sure I would have told him any sooner how I felt about Finn. Because I'm still finding all that out for myself. I do eventually tell him everything, but not until I pretty much have it all figured out.

But on top of that, he isn't the person I would have gone to with this, not the first person, anyway. It would have been Dad. Dad was the person I would have gone to for everything this summer: feeling abandoned by Liam and having to compete with Melissa. What was happening with Finn. Even figuring out how to move on without him. It was always Dad.

Before Liam leaves for the doctor's office, he pulls me up from the bed and hugs me. I wrap my arms around him and just stand there for a minute. For the first time this summer, I actually feel like it's good to have him here. "Thanks," I whisper in his ear. He just nods and leaves.

Chapter 11

W hen I walk out onto the porch, Aunt Marion is sitting at her easel, painting. She has a photo attached to the easel's edge with a clothespin. It's a snapshot of our beach house. On the front porch, two little girls sit with ice cream cones and huge smiles on their faces. I know without asking the girls are Mom and Aunt Marion. You can tell by the clothes they're wearing it was taken not long after grandpa bought the beach house in the mid-eighties. Mom and Aunt Marion are each wearing T-shirts and fuzzy leggings in bright neon colors over black tights. Their hair is held in pigtails by bright yellow scrunchies. But Aunt Marion's painting is muted, mostly sepia colored. By simply changing the color, Aunt Marion's painting emphasizes just the two girls. How close they are. How they're family. Perhaps for the first time, I realize Aunt Marion is good at what she does.

As I drop into the swinging chair mounted to the ceiling she says, "Look who's up!"

"How long did I sleep?" As soon as Liam left for the doctor's, I decided I was too exhausted to do anything. So I pulled off my towel and climbed under my sheets.

"Oh, about five hours. It's almost four. Liam went to the beach. I told him to be back as soon as they close the beach at five."

"Why?" I ask.

"Well, for one," she says, still not looking up from her easel, "I told him he was grounded. And so are you, for a night. No going out with your friends tonight. Both of you have pushed curfew too many nights this week." She puts the brush down and gives me her full attention. "Actually, two a.m. is not pushing curfew, it's breaking it. I didn't tell your mom, and quite frankly I don't want to. I think it's best if you and I have a conversation and be done with it. I know things are hard now, Tyler. I do. But staying out all night doesn't make it easier. And if you don't start coming home on time, you'll be missing more than one night of hanging out with your friends."

I nod but don't say anything. I'm not surprised she figured it out. And to be honest, I'm so exhausted that having a reason to stay in tonight is okay with me.

"And what's two?" I ask.

She returns to her painting and says, "Tonight, you, me, Liam, and your mom are going to Cape May for dinner. I decided you two can fit one evening into your busy schedules for the two ladies in your life you've known the longest." She mixes more paints on her palette.

"I'm surprised you talked Mom into going," I finally say.

Aunt Marion raises an eyebrow at me. "Why?"

I shrug. "I just thought Mom didn't feel like doing much of anything. That's all."

"Well, I guess you thought wrong."

I rock on the porch swing, and Aunt Marion drinks her lemonade. Ever since Aunt Marion and Liam arrived, Mom and I haven't really spent much time with each other, at least not alone. I'm not avoiding Mom, but being alone together doesn't really seem to help either of us. Once I got back from the hospital, I was still on crutches and couldn't move around by myself very well, so Mom never left me alone. She sat outside the bathroom door whenever I took a shower, afraid I might fall. She ordered groceries online, and the doorman offered to take out and pick up our dry cleaning. It felt like there was more room in our condo when Dad was there with us compared to after he died.

We also didn't talk to each other. I mean, we did talk, like saying good morning and stuff. But we didn't really ever say anything to each other. Each night at dinner, we would sit and eat silently while this giant emptiness seemed to consume our lives. Afterwards we would watch a movie and I usually fell asleep because of my pain pills. But we never really said much. The more time we spent together, the more we realized Dad was never coming back. Dad's death seemed to rip a hole between us that we couldn't fill.

I think Mom felt like she was suffocating too, because after I finished my physical therapy and the doctor said I was fine to walk and run and do everything like before, we came straight to the beach. We landed in Philadelphia, Mom rented a car, and we drove straight to Stone Harbor. After we unloaded the car, we sat on the porch. I had a lemonade and Mom drank a glass of white wine. After we sat in silence most of the evening, Mom finally stood up and said, "Maybe here, people will stop looking at me like I'm a helpless widow." Then she kissed me good night and went to bed. I knew exactly what she meant. Like me, she was tired of people constantly treating her like the poor woman whose husband just died. Mom and I are in the same spot. We both just want to move on, if someone would just give us the chance.

As I watch Aunt Marion paint, it dawns on me that she is the only person who doesn't treat me or Mom with gentle hands. I thought Aunt Marion was just like everyone else, trying to pretend nothing happened. Now I understand she's wasn't ignoring the fact that Dad died but was just making do without him being here. She called Spencer and had the Tribune come get all of Dad's files. She sat down with Mom and me and went through Dad's closet, making us pick out things we wanted to keep and things we would donate. She answered the landline and emphatically told all the interviewers and accident lawyers to leave us alone or she would get a restraining order. She's the one who actually got us to have the seafood dinner. I mean, it was pretty much a fiasco, but as bad as it was, I think in some way it was important we did it. Because the seafood dinner is just part of us coming to Stone Harbor.

And now that I think about it, Aunt Marion was the one who decided she and Liam would spend the whole summer here, instead of heading back to Baltimore after two weeks like they usually do. In a strange way, Aunt Marion is the reason Mom and I aren't just sitting on the beach, being alone together.

"So, what is your mom supposed to feel like doing now that your dad is gone?" She brushes a glob of brown paint onto the canvas.

"What?"

"You said you didn't think your mom felt much like doing anything now. So, I just wondered what she should feel like doing, in your opinion."

I shrug. "Something? Anything she wants. Whatever she feels like, I guess. I mean, she hasn't really said, so how am I supposed to know?" I've seen Aunt Marion do this with Liam enough to know that she's asking me this question to let me know I'm essentially doing something wrong. Or maybe not doing what needs to be done. She never really comes right out and says what you should be doing; instead, she makes you figure it out for yourself.

"Well, I do happen to know exactly how your mom is feeling right now. Actually, I've known almost all summer how she's been feeling."

"So, you're saying I should go up and ask Mom?" I drag my feet to stop the swing.

"That's probably the best decision you have made all summer," Aunt Marion says. Then she looks at me and gives a crooked smile. "And while you are up there, ask her if she would like to have dinner at Cape May tonight."

I knock on Mom's door, but before she even answers, I turn the knob. Mom is sitting up in bed, a copy of the Economist turned upside down in her lap.

"Hey, sweetie." She smiles.

"Hey. Are you sleeping?"

"Oh no. Just sitting here, I guess. How was your nap?"

I walk to the foot of her bed and sit down with my back to her, looking out the window at the ocean in the distance. Dad's aftershave still lingers in the air. It has been over a year since he was last here. I wonder how smells can linger for so long. It takes me back to the sports banquets after the cross-country season, and Dad would come straight from work. Dressed in a suit and the evening paper tucked under his arm, the smell of his aftershave was mild and pleasant. I always wondered if he put more aftershave on right before coming to the banquet or if it had lasted all day. From the scent in the air, I know now it lasted all day. Turns out, it lasted a year.

"Aunt Marion wants us to all go to dinner in Cape May tonight." I pull my phone from my pocket and look at the time. "In about an hour, I think. You want to go?"

"It's up to you."

I cringe and want to shout, I asked you first, so you tell me. Instead, I flop onto the bed and tilt my head back to look at her. She reaches down and strokes my hair.

"It was one of Dad's favorite places to eat," she says. "He loved taking us there, remember? Every year, we would have to go and have dinner, at least once. Sometimes more. Maybe we should go." I'm about to tell her I'm okay with this decision, but she adds, "Would you like that? Would it make you happy?"

I let out a deep sigh. "Mom, please don't ask me that. I'm not sure what I want. But I know I don't want everyone to keep asking me that."

She stops stroking my hair, and we sit in silence for a couple of minutes.

"Your dad always knew how to figure out what we wanted," Mom says, more to herself than to me. "Or at least he was good at getting us to tell him what we would like to do. That was his gift, you know. To get people to talk. It was so easy with him."

"I know," I say. Dad always joined us at the coach's circle after our cross-country meets. He was the only parent who would do that, or possibly could do that and not have Coach or the rest of the team feel he was out of place. Sometimes he was the one who started the conversation. What did we think about the race? What about the course? What about the hills or the narrow path under the trees? Back in the car, he and I would continue talking. What did I think about my race? Was there something I wanted to focus on, something I needed to improve before the next meet?

On those rare occasions when Mom would pick me up, she would wait by the car. As we drove home I would tell her what Coach had said, but never in detail, just a sentence or two. It wasn't that I felt like she didn't care. She always asked me how it all went. But we never had long conversations like I did with Dad.

"He used to ask me about everything. My day, school, what book I was reading. Everything. Sometimes I felt like he was interrogating me. Sometimes I wished he just didn't ask. But not that often. He always made it fun, you know?"

"That was what your dad did. He was good at getting people to talk. I guess because it was part of his job." She smiles. "But he did that with you because he really loved you. I think he would be really hurt to hear that sometimes you didn't want to talk. Was it a burden?"

"Are you kidding? Not at all. Most of the time I wanted to tell him things before anyone else knew, even before I could call Liam or tell one of my friends. When I had the best race, I wanted Dad to be the first one to know. When I got my first trophy, I wanted Dad to be the first one to hold it." It dawns on me that perhaps Mom knew all this already and maybe resented me for confiding in Dad first.

"I know, Tyler. I think your dad was your best friend . . . or as best a friend a dad can be with his son. I had all your life to watch this." She strokes my hair again. "I love you, Tyler. But I can't be like Dad. I can't replace him for you. He always knew what you were going through, sometimes without you even telling him—when you were anxious about a race, or a test, or upset about something. He just could read everyone. Including me. I got so comfortable with him knowing what was bothering me without having to actually tell him."

She pulls her knees up and wraps her arms around them as she sighs. "Sometimes the only reason I knew what was bothering you was because he figured it out and told me. Then I knew how to help you, how to come talk to you about it. Without him, I'm sure there would have been times when you and I would have never talked about what was wrong. You wouldn't have told me, and I would have never asked."

I pull myself up and sit next to her with my back against the headboard. She reaches down and grabs my hand, giving it a hard squeeze. "Neither one of us has that anymore. Sometimes you will just have to tell me what's wrong. And I will have to do the same for you. From here on out, the rules are a little different. He isn't here to . . . translate one another for us anymore." She wipes a tear that made its way down my cheek. "But I love you. And I need you. And I want to know how to make this easier for you, and how to help make you happy again. So, when I ask what you want, it is my way of doing what Dad could do without ever asking. Okay?"

I squeeze her hand. "Okay," I say. "Because I don't want to go to Cape May tonight for dinner."

We both laugh because we both know this isn't exactly what she was talking about, but it works.

"Good," Mom chuckles. "I didn't either. But if you had said yes, then I would have. God, that would have been horrible."

After I leave Mom's room, I tell Aunt Marion we aren't going to Cape May. When she asks what we are doing for dinner, I just shrug.

We eventually order pizza, sit on the porch, and talk. Mom hangs around after dinner a little longer than usual, and we play cards. Since coming to the shore this summer, it was the most we've felt like a family again—at least to me. We still aren't back to normal, but there is no going back to normal. We just have to figure out what comes next for us.

Chapter 12

The next day, Liam and I hang out on the beach. We both leave our phones at home, kind of an unspoken agreement that today is about us spending time together. Essentially, we finally catch each other up on what we've been doing all summer. Which is weird, given we've been living in the same house the entire time. I tell Liam about surfing with Finn, and we laugh as I get to the part about his swimsuit being ripped off me.

Then Liam starts to tell me about Melissa. How he knew he liked her from that time we first saw her playing volleyball. And he admits that, yes, he did tell her about Dad's death and the accident as a way to break the ice. I tell him that's okay.

As he talks, I think back to what he had said yesterday. How he's been dying to tell me how he feels about her. It's obvious that she makes him happy. So I'm happy for him. I say I do like her, but her constant habit of jumping and clapping kind of annoys me. He laughs and says he knows. I don't hide it very well. I make a mental note to try and give her more of a break.

I also point out that she always comes up with these plans to make sure the evenings end with her and Liam being alone, and sometimes it would be nice if they hung out with all of us. It's my way of saying that I need him. Not to help me remember Dad, I'll be able to do that on my own. I need him like I needed Dad. Someone to talk to, help me figure things out. To share what I'm going through. Which means if Liam is willing to be there like that for me, I have to start making sure I'm there for him too.

When we finally head back up to the beach house, Liam has at least ten messages from Melissa. He shrugs and says, "I'll call her later, after you and I decide what we want to do for dinner." Then he disappears upstairs to the bathroom, and I head to the shower outside.

For dinner we go to Pizza Open, and Liam muses how he never knew about it. For some reason I feel kind of proud that I'm showing him something new about Stone Harbor. We decide to go to the boardwalk afterwards.

As we drive to Wildwood, Liam finally calls Melissa to tell her we will meet at the boardwalk and then find something to do. I tap the steering wheel, waiting for the Egg Harbor drawbridge to come back down. Then Liam says, "Hang on, Melissa, I need to check on something."

I look at him.

"So, do you want us to go find Finn tonight too? Or do you want to just hang with me and Melissa? It's up to you, but I thought I'd ask."

I think for a second about spending the evening alone with them. And although Melissa's clapping and giggling still make me cringe, I figure I can handle being with them tonight, for Liam's sake.

But I also think about Finn. We haven't texted or called or anything. I want to talk to him, but I'm not sure how he feels or what he wants. The only way to know is to ask. Which means we at least need to find out if he wants to join us tonight. He might not be interested, but if so, that's okay. At least we gave him the option.

"Yeah, I want to see him," I finally respond to Liam.

Liam turns back to the phone. "Hey, babe. Why don't you

just meet us at the shooting gallery." After a long pause, he says, "No really, it's okay. Seriously."

By the time we find a parking spot and walk to the shooting gallery, Melissa is already there. As we approach, it's obvious Finn isn't working.

"Is he off tonight?" Liam asks as we get close, but Melissa puts her fingers to her mouth and shushes us.

"No," Melissa whispers. "I called his house after I talked to you because when I called his phone it went straight to voicemail. His mom said he was at work. But when I got here"—Melissa motions to the girl we saw before working in the gallery—"she said he called in sick."

We all stand silent for a moment, wondering what to do. Then Liam says, "You didn't tell him I was coming, did you? Maybe he's avoiding me."

"No," Melissa says with exasperation, "I haven't spoken to him since, like, two days ago. That's why I called his house."

"Okay, fine," Liam says, waving his hands.

"Look," I finally say. "We were just wondering if you have any idea where he might be. I mean, he is your friend."

"Yeah, but he's your . . . " Melissa catches herself short. "Friend too. And he and I are not, like, best friends. I mean, I see him for two months in the summer, and I've only known him for two years."

"Okay. Let's forget Finn then," Liam says as he puts his arm around Melissa to try to settle her down. "What do we want to do? It'll get dark soon."

Suddenly I have an idea—and a guess as to where Finn might be. "Follow me," I say and head down the boardwalk.

"Where are we going?" Melissa asks but doesn't move.

"We need to get sparklers," I say. I look over my shoulder at Liam.

A huge smile breaks across his face as he grabs Melissa by the hand. "Come on," he says. "This is going to be fun."

Years ago, Dad would take Liam and me to the Cape May Lighthouse and let us run along the beach with sparklers. He would always make it a special event. On some random day after lunch, he would announce, "We boys need to go down to Hoy's five-and-dime to do some shopping." He would buy us each a box of sparklers, and we would plan to go to Cape May a day or two later. Sometimes Liam and I couldn't wait, and we would beg him to let us each have one sparkler that day.

"Once, Tyler and I got ahold of the whole bag, and we ran around the porch in the middle of the afternoon playing with them," Liam tells Melissa as we drive down to Cape May after finding sparklers in a 7-Eleven store just off the boardwalk. He's driving, with Melissa in the passenger seat, and I'm in the back. "We had to go buy another box to take to Cape May."

"Your dad wasn't mad?"

"No," I answer. "I mean, we were maybe six or seven. He just told us next time we would have to learn to be patient, and if we used them all during the day then we would have none to take to the lighthouse at night."

As we pull into the parking lot for the Cape May Lighthouse, we see Finn's car, and my stomach drops a little. I'm not sure why I wanted to see him tonight, and now that I'm going to, I'm anxious.

"Good call, Ty," Liam says as he turns off the car and climbs out.

Melissa gets out of the passenger side, holding the bag of sparklers. "How did you know he would be here?"

I shrug. I'm not about to tell either of them how much time he and I have spent here this summer sitting on the ruins watching the ferries go by. He told me that this was one of his favorite things to do when he needed to just escape from everyone. I knew there was a good chance he would be here now since the sun is just about to set and the ferries will be lit up as they cruise by. I just took a gamble. We round the path through the dunes and hit the beach. Liam stops and exclaims, "Wow. I forgot what this place was like. It's been ages." He holds Melissa's hand and they just stand there, looking around.

"This way," I call without stopping and head toward the ruins. As I come up from behind them, I see Finn sitting in the sand with his back up against the bunkers. He is wearing the same green shirt he wore when I first met him. His knees are pulled up to his chest, and his arms are wrapped around his shins.

"Hey," I call out as I get close, softly so I wouldn't spook him. He turns toward me. That smile I've spent months admiring creeps across his face, and he calls back as he slowly stands. He shoves his hands in his back pockets and cocks his head to one side. I smile back. Then, from behind me, Liam and Melissa round the corner of the ruins, laughing. Finn's smile instantly breaks, and he gives me a quizzical look. Liam and Melissa nearly knock me over, and when they see Finn, both go suddenly silent.

After an awkward pause, Liam finally says, "Hey."

"Hey," Finn nods, but he is rightfully leery.

"Look, I was thinking, maybe we can just forget . . ." Liam starts. Then he rubs his hands slowly down his face, and says, "Actually, let me start again. I was out of line. Way out of line. And well, you . . . you punched me. I would have done the same thing. Except not, like, in the ear." He laughs, and it breaks the tension enough that we all giggle.

"Honestly," Liam continues, "I have nothing against you. I was upset about something stupid between me and Ty, and I pulled you into it. I shouldn't have, and I'm sorry. I like you, you're a cool dude. I know you're a really good friend of Tyler's, and you were there for him when . . . well, when I wasn't. And for that I'm grateful." Liam extends his hand, and as he patiently waits for Finn to shake it, he adds, "And I'm sorry for what I said."

"I like you too, Liam," Finn says. "You seem like a good guy, and what you said was out of line. I think that's why it really hurt. But I think, deep down, you're a good guy . . . just not that night." Finn still hasn't taken Liam's hand. "And I do feel bad I hit you in the ear."

"Yeah, I know. Tyler told me you said you were sorry about it."

Finn looks at me with surprise. He never told me that, because we haven't spoken since that night.

"Well," I quickly jump in. "It was all so messed up, and I think I said everyone felt bad about it."

This is good enough for Finn, at least for now, because he grabs Liam's hand and shakes it.

There is a palpable sense of relief in the air. Then Melissa exclaims, "Look, we brought sparklers!" She hands each of us a box.

"Sparklers?" Finn asks, somewhat befuddled as he turns the box in his hand.

"Tradition," I say.

Not missing a beat, Liam says, "We go down to the water's edge and just run around and have fun as the sun sets and the tide comes in. We did this years ago when we were kids, with Tyler's dad. Want to join us, Finn?"

"Why don't you two go," I say. "We'll join you in a second."

"Okay," Melissa says, and quickly heads further down the beach.

Liam lingers for a second. "Well, okay. But I kind of wanted . . . "

"I know," I say, anticipating what he's about to say next. "We're coming. Just don't use them all before we get there."

Liam turns and leaves, and suddenly it's awkward again. Finn leans back against the bunkers and looks at me. "So," he said. "You told him I was sorry."

"I think what I said was that you were upset. That's all. I think he just interpreted it as an apology. But the rest is true. None of what was going on between me and Liam had anything to do with you. You just kind of got caught in the crossfire."

A ferry honks in the distance. I motion toward the top of the ruins, and Finn and I scramble up. We watch in silence as the ferry slowly appears around the tip of the cape.

"You know, Liam was right," Finn says as he takes a deep breath. "That is, about how I felt . . . that I like you . . . like that. And I thought maybe you liked me too. But I wasn't sure if you were . . . " He turns away from me.

"I know," I say, and take a step closer so I'm directly behind him. I put my head on his shoulder and say in his ear, "Me too."

"Really?"

"I just . . . wasn't sure how I felt, at first."

"But now?"

I sigh. "Now I'm not sure I know that much more, really."

"Oh. So, you're saying you're not . . . " His voice trails off.

That wasn't the right thing to say. But I'm not sure I can say it much better. Everything has been confusing about this summer, and there is no simple answer. Even if Dad were here, this is something I'd have to figure out on my own. I owe Finn some answer though, so I do my best.

"Look, I know that I like being with you. And talking to you. And surfing with you."

He laughs.

"Okay, trying to surf. But anyway, I like you. Right now, you're the only one who makes me feel . . ." I need a moment to figure out what to say next. Finally, the words come to me. "You're like running, you know? You are the only one who makes me feel anything. Period. With you, everything feels more, and I like it. I like you. So, call me whatever you want, because that's how I feel."

I put my arms over his shoulders. He leans back into my arms, and his head falls snugly under my chin. My heart races wildly, and I wonder if he can feel it. The ferry is almost gone now. The sun has just gone down, and the lights on the ferry pop out so we can just follow it as it keeps chugging across the bay. As we silently watch it pull away, I count two weeks until I have to head back to Chicago. That is if I want to start pre-season for cross-country.

"So, what do we do now?" Finn asks. In the distance, I hear Melissa giggling and clapping. I physically cringe, and I know Finn feels this because he laughs and pats my hand.

"You guys! Tyler! Finn! Hurry up and get down here," Liam yells.

I step away from Finn and grab his hand.

"Now? Let's go down to the beach."

About the Author

Garth A. Fowler lives, runs, and writes in Chicago. Prior to moving to Chicago, he lived in Seattle where he received a PhD in behavioral neuroscience at the University of Washington. Since then, he has had numerous jobs including being a triathlon coach, a biomedical researcher, and a professor. He has published scientific papers, articles, and book chapters on visual neuroscience, cognition, attention, and the career preparation of young scientists. *Calm Undone* is his debut novel.

Acknowledgements

Thanks to my family—my parents and my brothers and sisters. *Calm Undone* is about family, and I'm lucky to have you as mine. Special thanks to Grandma, who insisted that our entire family (cousins, aunts, and uncles) gather each year in Stone Harbor for a family vacation. Those days are some of the best memories I have of growing up.

The first chapter of this book was written in a coffee shop on Fifteenth Avenue in Capitol Hill, Seattle, where I often hung out with a group of misfits like myself. Thanks to the Seattle Posse (you know who you are). Thanks to Steph, who misheard me when I told her the original title of the book and hence came up with *Calm Undone*. It's a much better name.

Thanks to BQB Publishing for guiding me through the process of publishing my first book. Finally, thanks to Andrea Vande Vorde and Allison Itterly, whose comments, suggestions, and questions pushed me to make Tyler, Liam, Finn, and the rest of the characters come to life.